Lock Down Publications and Ca$h
Presents

I0680383

FRESH
OFF DA
PORCH

THE TALE OF A KNUCKLEHEAD

Written By

IRA B.

First Edition 2025

Printed in the United States of America

Lock Down Publications
P.O. Box 944
Stockbridge, GA 30281
www.lockdownpublications.com

Like our page on Facebook: Lock Down Publications
www.facebook.com/lockdownpublications.ldp

Stay Connected with Us!

Text **LOCKDOWN** to 22828 to stay up-to-date with new releases, sneak peaks, contests and more...

Like our page on Facebook:
Lock Down Publications

Join Lock Down Publications/The New Era Reading Group

Visit our website:
www.lockdownpublications.com

Follow us on Instagram:
Lock Down Publications

Email Us: We want to hear from you!

Dedication

I dedicate this book to the young and most beautiful Zoe Oli, the little CEO of beautiful Curly Me. I salute you, little boss lady. Keep promoting the love and positivity in your community. I see bigger success in your future. You are something special, and I'm proud of you.

Chapter 1

Quincy, FL.

It was a beautiful autumn day in the hood. Niggas were booming good in their traps, bitches were turning heads and showing off their essence, and the kids were all over the place, getting into all kinds of shit.

Just another typical day in the hood.

Everything was kosher.

But not with young Cody Williams. He was mad as hell, and he didn't want to be around anybody. While all his friends were out there having a good time without him, he was in the house, sulking. Once again, his mother had let him down and wasn't upholding her word as a woman. Cody didn't have any understanding of that, especially when it was his seventeenth birthday, and he didn't have what was promised to him.

"Cody!" shouted his mother, Tami, who was home for the fourth day in a row now from her job at the local hair salon. He knew she had been fired due to her not showing up on time to fulfill her duties and public intoxication. And she stole. Cody knew what it was though, and it had a lot to do with that so-called nigga she was seeing. His name was Wesley Peacock from over in the Sub-Division area, and it was his fault that Tami was strung out on molly. Ever since he introduced her to that shit, she hadn't been the same, always up for days and crashing hard and never being able to look out for Cody like she used to.

The new Air Jordans that she'd promised to get him for his birthday tomorrow, Cody knew he wouldn't be seeing those shoes for a long time. At least not on his feet he wouldn't. All he wanted was the new Jays and not the busted-up Nikes he had now.

"Cody!? Bring your little, black ass here, dammit!" Tami yelled from her bedroom up the hall.

Cody had been sitting by the window in his own room, looking outside and longing for a reason to smile. He sucked his teeth and got up to go see what his mother wanted.

"I know you heard me callin' your ass the first time," said Tami when he suddenly appeared in her bedroom doorway. "What are you doing, Cody?" she asked.

"Nothing," he answered simply.

"Well, I need you to go buy me some cigarettes from Linda," she said, referring to the hood's candy lady who sold just about anything the hood desired. Tami reached from her lying down position in bed for the money she had lying on the nightstand. "Tell Linda I said the other five is what I owe her from last time," she said.

Cody approached the bed and took the ten-dollar bill that she offered him.

"And come your ass right back too," she said.

"I am," he told her. Cody couldn't believe she had the audacity to use the money to buy cigarettes and give away to someone else instead of putting it toward his birthday gift.

He took the money and left the room without a backward glance or any further reply.

Back inside his room, he stepped into his busted-up shoes. Cody hated those shoes; they were last year's shoes. Grudgingly, he put them on and made his way for the front door to take his leave.

Lord knows he didn't want to go outside.

He wasn't in the mood.

But he would do anything for his mother, no matter how selfishly self-centered she was.

6

~   ~   ~

Fifteen minutes later, Cody was on his way back home from the candy lady's house with a pack of Newport shorts plus a pickled egg that he was in the process of demolishing. Linda was cool people. She was for the struggle.

As he walked along the sidewalk of Key Street, headed home where his misery laid, Cody contemplated over what he wanted to do for his birthday tomorrow. There damn sure wouldn't be a party nor would he have his Air Jordans, so he would have to think of something to do that was worthwhile.

But all that came to a screeching halt when Cody looked over to his right and saw Ms. Donna struggling to bend down to pick something up off the ground of her front yard. Ms. Donna was one of the elderly women in the hood who wasn't all stuck-up and bad-tempered like all the others. She too was for the people and lived to cater to those who had her best interest at heart. So, when Cody saw that she was having a hard time, he made it his business to intervene.

"What's up, Ms. Dee? You need help wit' something?" Cody asked, stepping over into her front yard.

"Just tryna pick up enough pecans to bake my pie," she said. Ms. Donna was in her late sixties, petite, and still beautiful, despite her bad back and weakened knees.

Observing the situation before him, Cody saw that she had a plastic Wal-Mart shopping bag in one hand and a couple of pecans in the other. She dropped the pecans into the bag and bent forward to gather up some more.

"Hold up! You don't have to do that, Ms. Dee." Cody approached her and laid a hand upon her arm to stop her.

"I can handle it, my boy!"

"No," he said firmly. "I'll do it for you."

"Really? You'll pick 'em up for me?" Ms. Donna looked hopeful.

He nodded.

The ground was laden with fallen pecans from the huge pecan tree sprouted from the earth in the middle of the front yard. There were hundreds of them spread about the lawn. He took the bag from her and began picking up the pecans.

"You are wonderful," she said to him. "I'll be in the kitchen when you're finished."

"How many should I pick?"

"You'll know when enough is enough, my boy. Thank you." Ms. Donna hurried back inside her house and shut the door behind her.

Right then, a group of young boys shot past the house on their bikes and laughed out loud. Cody looked up at them and envied their joyousness, wishing his own bike was operational enough for him to ride it. He sighed in exasperation and resumed his task of picking pecans. But little did he know that that one simple act was about to introduce him to a whole other hustle.

One that would change the game.

~   ~   ~

"Cody!" bellowed Tami from way up the street. At the sound of his name, Cody looked up and saw his mother standing outside their house on the front porch.

"Damn!" muttered Cody, having taken on another task before completing the initial one. He had forgotten all about his mother's pack of cigarettes.

After abandoning what was left of his pickings, Cody hurried up the street toward his house. And of course, Tami didn't move a muscle nor did she look happy to see him at the moment. Cody made his journey over to her and delivered the pack of cigarettes with the humility of someone expecting to be chastised.

Tami snatched the Newports from him and wasted no time breaking its seal. "What the hell you over there doing in that woman's yard?"

"I was helping Ms. Donna," he said.

"Helping her do what?" Tami stuck a cigarette between her lips and lit up.

"Pickin' up pecans," said Cody.

"Is she paying you to pick 'em?"

He shrugged. "Maybe," he replied. Tami gave him that side-eye of hers that he knew so well. He braced himself for a verbal reprimand, but it didn't come. It was more of a compliment than anything.

"Well, I raised you right. It's good that you're helping her. It's about time you find something to do other than stinking up the house all day," said Tami. "And always remember, hard work deserves a good payment. It's about time you start helpin' out with the bills."

Cody watched his mother turn around and walk away in her tight-fitting booty shorts. He shook his head and hurried back to Ms. Donna's house.

There were three bags of pecans sitting on the ground under the tree. Cody had gotten carried away with his pickings. He wanted to impress the old lady, and besides, he didn't have anything better to do with his time.

"Oh, my," said Ms. Donna in surprise when she opened the back door to the kitchen to find Cody standing there hefting three bulging bags of pecans. "You are so amazing, my boy! This is wonderful. Come. I have a treat for you." She smiled sweetly.

The treat was her taking the time to show him the fundamentals on how to bake a pecan pie. They spent their time unshelling the pecans, processing the baking materials, and then came the pies, baked to perfection and crispy with delight.

"For your efforts, I've baked you two pies for yourself and here is ten dollars." Ms. Donna reached into her apron pocket and handed him the money.

"Thank you, Ms. Dee," he said.

"You know, Claire, from over yonder by the park, she would love it if you could help her out too," Ms. Donna suggested. "She will pay you handsomely if you're willing to lend a hand."

"What does she need done?"

"The same as me. The senior ball is coming up, and it's our job to bake pies and such. Claire and I are the ones for the task," she exclaimed.

"I'll see," he said. Cody pocketed his money and stared down at the two pies in front of him on the kitchen counter. Then, he gazed out the kitchen window to see that nightfall was near. "I gotta go."

"I know," she said. "Thank you, Cody. And don't become a stranger, ya hear?"

"I won't," he promised.

Cody grabbed his two pies, and with one healthy sigh, he headed for the door. He was grateful for the old ladies providing him with a way to earn some money. At least he wouldn't be broke for his birthday tomorrow, plus he had a nice homemade pecan pie to celebrate with. Cody considered himself lucky, but luck for him was about to take him to the next level.

Chapter 2

He was two houses down from his house when a black on black '23 BMW XM Label SUV pulled up to a halt at the curb next door to his childhood home. Cody, with both pecan pies stacked on top of one another, looked up as three doors from the SUV opened.

It was Twan and his two loyal homeboys, Dale and Rod. The house where they had just arrived to belonged to Twan's sister, Alisha, who, to her brother's credible reputation, was the one who supplied the area with the best weed in town. Cody liked Alisha; she was always good to him, and he would do just about anything to please her.

"Young C, what you got there, my nigga?" said Twan as he stepped onto the sidewalk into Cody's path. He was decked from head to toe in his usual dope-boy attire and dripping in iced out jewels.

"Some pecan pies Ms. Dee made for me," Cody said.

"What? You sellin' them or something?" asked Rod, coming up alongside of Twan with a sizzling blunt of loud between his fingers.

"I'm not sellin' them," said Cody.

"You say Ms. Donna the one who made them?" Twan asked, and Cody nodded his head. "Damn. That old lady right there is a beast wit' baking pies."

"Oh, yeah?" said Dale.

Twan nodded.

"Lemme buy one then," Rod said to Cody, reaching into the pocket of his Ralph Lauren jeans for the thick knot of cash he had there.

"I'll buy the other one too," said Dale.

"Hold the fuck up, niggas! If anybody gonna cop one of them, it should be me," Twan replied.

"Home team advantage, huh?"

Twan smirked.

"I got ten dollars for one right now," Dale offered.

"I got twenty," said Rod, peeling off a twenty dollar bill from the cash in his hand.

Cody looked up at Twan and, without saying a word, offered him one of the pies. Twan reached for the top dish and at the same time reached into his pants pocket, but instead of pulling out money, Twan extracted a Zip-loc bag of molly and handed it to him.

"What's this?" asked Cody.

"That's a half ounce of molly, Young C."

"How much is it worth?"

When Twan gave him a quick estimate, Cody's eyes widened with surprise. "This is how you earn your keep," said Twan. "Holla at me when you ready for more."

"This nigga always stuntin' on a muthafucker," Rod replied. "It ain't nothing but a fuckin' pie!"

"It's more than just a pie, brah," Twan told him, now holding the dish with both hands.

"What's up wit' that other one?" Dale asked. He was one of those big, stocky niggas, and it was evident he was high off weed; therefore, he had the munchies and wanted to feed his high.

"I'm not sellin' it," Cody told him.

Twan laughed and walked away toward the front door of his sister's house.

"Ain't shit fuckin' funny, nigga," Rod said as he took off after him. "You gon' give me some of that pie."

That was when the streetlights came on, and Cody knew he had better make it home.

A minute later, he walked through the front door of his house. Upon his entrance, he was struck with three things that gave him mixed emotions. The first being the smell of fried chicken, then the sound of the headboard smacking the wall in his mother's bedroom as her and Wesley fucked noisily, and then, the unmistakable stench of weed laced with molly permeating the air around him. Cody turned up his nose and headed into the kitchen where his dinner awaited in the microwave.

While demolishing his chicken, yellow rice, and sweet peas, Cody contemplated over the matter he was now faced with. He had ten dollars and a half ounce of molly. How could he turn that into the money he needed to purchase his Jordans overnight? And why didn't Twan just give him the money instead of product? Didn't he know Cody knew nothing about selling drugs, only that his mother was a mollyhead and her boyfriend was as well, which meant that he couldn't trust them to do what needed to be done in his favor?

By the time Cody finished his meal, with a healthy slice of pecan pie, he had convinced himself he could accomplish his task before his birthday.

"I see you finally made it back home," said Tami the second Cody rinsed off the dish and fork and turned toward the kitchen doorway.

"I see Wesley is back again too," said Cody. "I thought you dumped him, Mama?"

From her velvet housecoat, Tami reached into the pocket for her cigarettes. "We found a way to make it work. Now, did Donna pay you?"

Hesitantly, he nodded and told her, "I'm gonna put it toward my birthday gift tomorrow."

"And what's that?"

"What I've been beggin' you for all along."

"The Air Jordans?"

He nodded.

Tami lit her cigarette and said, "You and those damn shoes. I guess we'll have to see what tomorrow brings, huh?" She opened the fridge and brought out the pitcher of Kool-Aid. "I see Donna made you your own personal pecan pie."

"You can have a piece if you want some."

"Maybe later," she said. Cody watched as she grabbed two glasses from the cabinet. He then walked out of the kitchen for his bedroom.

Inside his room, Cody sat on the edge of his bed and pulled out the bag of molly.

"I'ma see what Teddy know about this," he said to himself. Teddy Anderson was one of his closest friends, whose big brother, Money Mel, was a drug dealer. Teddy claimed that on occasions, he would sell crack and flakka for his brother when Money Mel was not able to do so because he would be out of town or simply not available to cater to his customers.

The last thing Cody wanted was to be a drug dealer, so he had to figure out a plan because just holding the product wouldn't get him anywhere.

He trusted Teddy for the job.

Cody was sure this was the right plan.

Tomorrow, he would indeed have his Air Jordans — or else he would never forgive himself.

~   ~   ~

It was some time after nine p.m. when Cody came knocking on Teddy's bedroom window. He had snuck out of his own bedroom window to make the journey two streets over to Teddy's house.

Teddy was in the process of gliding through the social media sites on his cell phone while munching on a Star Crunch pastry. He looked over to the window at the sound.

Teddy was of the chubby stature, a very round sixteen-year-old hoodlum, the very same one who influenced Cody to take his first hit of weed when he was eleven. When Teddy made it to the window and saw who it was, he gestured toward the back of the house.

Moments later, the back door opened, and Cody hurriedly stepped inside. To Teddy, his friend seemed overly anxious, so he took it upon himself to step forward and scan the area outside behind the house.

"You okay, Cody?" he asked after not finding anything worth troubling over. Teddy was always protective over Cody, like a big brother would be to his younger sibling.

"I'm okay," he said.

"What's up then?" Teddy dapped him up.

"Gotta show you something."

"What?"

When Cody said nothing and was en route to Teddy's room, Teddy followed close behind and locked the door behind them when they went inside.

Cody pulled out the bag of molly and handed it over to Teddy. "What is this?"

"A half of zip."

"Zip?" Cody gave him a puzzled look.

"An ounce, Cody. Don't you know anything? All that shit Mama Tami be poppin' and smokin', you should know what this is." Teddy caught the stern look his friend gave him and said, "My bad, brah. I shouldn't have said that shit."

With a nonchalant shrug, Cody then asked Teddy if he could sell it for him before tomorrow.

"Before tomorrow? That's impossible unless there's somebody out there fienin' for this shit right now," said Teddy. "And whoever that somebody is, I have to…" Teddy suddenly paused for a second, and Cody noticed the pensive expression forming upon his face.

"What, Teddy?"

"Big Boi," Teddy said with a start.

"What about him?"

Big Boi Conyers was an older gangster who lived not too far from where they stood. He was a friend of the family, Teddy's Aunt Lisa's ex-boyfriend who used to beat her ass. Big Boi owned a food truck business and was said to be a mean mollyhead. The only reason Teddy suggested him was because Big Boi still looked out for him when he could, and he was Tink Tink's uncle, Teddy's childhood sweetheart and the girl who he loved.

"Big Boi will buy all of this wit' no problem," said Teddy confidently.

"You think so?" Cody could see the excitement spewing from his friend.

"Let's go and find out."

Cody hesitated. "Right now?"

"Yeah."

After mulling over it for a moment, Cody thought back on how he was betraying his mother's trust by being out so late. But his commitment led him this far, so he may as well continue. He was on a mission to succeed, and by all means, he was determined to make it happen.

"Let's go," said Cody.

Now, it was Teddy's turn to hesitate, as he stared at Cody in astonishment.

"What?" Cody fidgeted with his LA Lakers snapback.

Teddy smirked. "You really want those shoes, huh, brah?" he replied.

Cody looked at him with a straight face, and then, he said, "Desperately. I don't care for nothing else except for that, Teddy."

"Say no more then," Teddy replied.

Cody was done talking. The only thing that mattered at that point was making money.

Chapter 3

"That's right, bitch. Swallow all that dick. You asked for it, so now you got it!" Big Boi was reclined in his seat, behind the wheel of his old school Monte Carlo. Face first in his lap was one of his regular tricks, Sugar Foot, who was deep throating his manhood like a champ. Big Boi was so into receiving such amazing oral service that he didn't see Cody and Teddy approach his car. He had no clue he was being watched because his head was back, and his eyes were closed in pleasure. That was a bad mistake for a thoroughbred gangster who lived to see fifty after creating his share of enemies. What he was doing at that moment was a quick way to get a bullet through your brain.

Fortunately for him, the two juvenile delinquents were not killers; they just lived amongst them. And sure enough, the Pepper Hill community was one of the deadliest spots in the small town.

And here it was, Big Boi was slacking instead of being on point like the old Big Boi used to be.

He was too comfortable.

"I'm 'bout to nut," he announced to Sugar Foot, his hand on the back of her head, stroking her hair and guiding her rhythm.

When he tensed up just before his release, Teddy gave three sharp knocks against the driver door window, startling them both.

"Oh, shit!" Big Boi looked up to see two faces peering in on him. In the process, Sugar Foot also lifted her head up, away from Big Boi's dick, just as he erupted. "No, fuck!" he cursed when he realized what had just happened. Instead of busting off down her throat, Big Boi now had a mess of semen soiling his clothes and the interior of the car.

"I'm sorry," said Sugar Foot, a twenty-year-old dope addict and hooker. She was younger than his own two grown children, but Big Boi did not give a damn.

A trick was a trick.

"I'll clean it up for you, Big Boi. Just lemme cut on the light real quick," she replied. Sugar Foot reached inside her purse for the red handkerchief she had there and switched on the dome light.

When the car was finally illuminated, it was then that Cody and Teddy saw the cold scowl etched on the gangster's face. Also in his left hand was a 357 Magnum, and the way he was looking, Big Boi would have no problem using it.

"What the fuck do you two knuckleheads want? Ain't it past your damn bedtime?" said Big Boi in that menacing tone of his.

"We got something good for you," Teddy answered.

"What you got?"

Cody watched as the OG sat there while Sugar Foot diligently wiped him up with the cloth as if it was no big deal. It wasn't the first time he witnessed someone getting their dick sucked; he walked in on his mother doing it to Wesley a few times. He hated it when that happened.

"When you done in there, then we can talk," Teddy told Big Boi before turning around and gesturing for his friend to follow suit.

Together, they distanced themselves from the car parked in the driveway for the front steps of Big Boi's home. Minutes ago, they had knocked on the front door of the house and got no answer, but Cody had spotted movement through the car window and headed in its direction.

Teddy said, "I should feel some type of way about that shit."

"Sugar Foot?" Cody spoke up.

He nodded. "It's like that nigga don't got no respect for my family. And Sugar Foot ain't makin' it no better, especially after knowing what Auntie Lisa had went through wit' him."

"So, what're you gonna do about it?"

Teddy gazed over at his friend. "What I'm gonna do about it?" he said. "I'ma tell him I don't appreciate that shit he doing."

"And she'll still keep doing what she do. Sugar Foot is too far gone, Teddy. You can't change somebody who don't wanna change."

"You sound like my daddy, brah."

"He's a smart man."

Teddy nudged him in the side with an elbow. "Shut up, fool. Here he come," he said.

The car door opened, and Big Boi climbed out like a bear emerging from a dark cave. On the other side, Sugar Foot got out and headed for the sidewalk and into the shadows of the night.

"This shit better be good," said Big Boi as he approached the front porch with his pistol still clutched in his grasp. It was legend that Big Boi was very handy with his gun. His reputation was solidified by his gangsterism, for he had come from an era where survival of the fittest was warranted.

Big Boi was official.

He wasn't the type to play games.

No real true killer did.

~   ~   ~

The half ounce of molly was now in Big Boi's hand as he examined its quantity. Standing in the living room of his home amongst him were his two young companions. Teddy delivered his sales pitch, and Cody assured him there was plenty more where that came from.

"What you want for this?" Big Boi asked.

"How much is it worth to you?"

Big Boi frowned. "Can't put a price on your shit, youngblood. Gimme a solid number and I'll see if I can cover it for you."

"You can," Teddy added knowingly. Once upon a time, Big Boi had been a millionaire after his small stint in the NFL, playing for the Denver Broncos. Then, the double-homicide happened, and all his money went into court fees, trying to beat his case. He ended up having to do five years in prison. It was just five years ago when he jacked some young hustler for his money and his product and used his profits to build from. Now, he was a successful business owner with a good savings account to keep him afloat.

And Big Boi was still a killer, no doubt about it. He just hadn't had the motivation to do it lately.

"Lemme see what you got right here." Big Boi opened the Zip-loc bag and reached inside for a molly rock. He put it in his mouth. Then, he scooped some molly dust onto a finger and snorted it up his nose.

Teddy and Cody looked at one another. Cody braced himself to snatch the bag of molly out of Big Boi's hand if he got too carried away. He wasn't just going to stand there and let him take advantage of his product without paying first.

"You got your tester. You see what it is. Now it's time to get down to business, Big Boi," said Teddy.

Cody said, "What'cha gon' do? Barbecue or mildew?" He had borrowed the saying from his mother. She had a habit of using it when her patience was running thin.

"I got you two hunnid right now for it," said Big Boi.

"It's a deal," Cody replied.

"Hell no!" Teddy objected and looked at the older gangster as if he'd lost his damn mind. "Stop playing games,

Big Boi. You know damn well that's worth more than two hundred. You gotta do better than that," he said.

"Whose dope is this, yours or his?"

"It don't matter, nigga, whose dope it is. We gon' do straight business," Cody told him. "And I'm not takin' nothing less than four hundred." It was Teddy's objection that made him respond the way he did.

"Take it or leave it, Big Boi," Teddy interjected.

Just as Big Boi opened his mouth to say something, the front door exploded open, and three armed goons came rushing inside. Before Big Boi could lift his pistol to take aim, automatic rounds rang out as four slugs punched him in the chest and stomach.

Instinctively, Cody took off running for the back of the house. He jetted down the nearby hallway for the back door. He expected to hear more gunshots or someone chasing after him. But neither came as he cleared the back door and darted into the darkness.

Cody ran all the way home.

He was scared out of his mind.

And even worse, Cody left without getting paid or his product. But at the moment, he didn't care about the molly or his Air Jordans. His only concern was making it home alive and in one piece.

Chapter 4

The following morning, Cody woke up to the sound of music booming from the sound system up front. He sat up in bed and yawned tiredly. Then came the sound of raised voices talking over the loud music. Cody recognized three of the voices almost instantly, then he proceeded to climb out of bed.

The night before, Cody had witnessed cold-blooded murder and ran for his life. After he made it home, Cody locked himself into the room. Fear of somebody kicking down his front door to kill him next made it hard for him to sleep last night. But that fate never came, then sleep finally claimed him some time after three o'clock. He was emotionally exhausted.

Now here it was, six hours later, and his body was still begging for more rest.

And that was when he saw the shoe box. It was perched on top of his dresser. It was protruding out of a large shopping bag from the Foot Locker shoe store. Cody felt his heart quicken with excitement and hurried over to the old, scarred dresser.

"The Jordan 12s," said Cody as emotion welled up in his chest. The colors were black and red, the very same Air Jordans he had been dying to have for the past several months. "She did it," he sighed. A crooked smile spread across his face as he checked the shoe size and saw that the number was accurate.

Up front, it sounded like a party was in progress, and Cody could only guess what he would find once he made his grand entrance.

Tami had a brand-new outfit laid out for him too. She had really kept her word, and Cody was grateful for that. Because he had doubted her, Cody had taken it upon himself to get the job done. And in the process, he almost lost his life because of it.

Cody did his best to remain humble about the whole situation. What he went through the night before was enough to make him out of a believer.

That the street game was not for him.

That he wasn't built for it.

All Cody wanted to do was go to school, play basketball, thrive in his goals that would shape his future, and then create a better life for his mother. Seeing Big Boi die the way he did last night really got his mind right.

Cody wondered how Teddy made it out last night. He was scared for his friend.

Teddy being as fat as he was, he wouldn't have gotten away fast enough, even if he tried. And Cody hated having to leave him behind, but he was left with no other choice. And besides, Cody was certain Teddy made it out alive or else he would have known by now.

Teddy was his brother from another mother, and his mother, Shequita, would have called Tami to make sure that Cody was alive and well.

With a shake of his head, Cody slipped over across the hall into the bathroom to take a quick shower. Today was his day, and by any means necessary, he was going to make this birthday a memorable one.

Fifteen minutes later, Cody was back in his bedroom and getting dressed in his new pair of Kapital jeans and its matching t-shirt. Then, with the patience of a killer, he stepped into his Air Jordans and strung them up, feeling like a brand-new man.

These were his first pair of Jays.

Cody was feeling himself.

But that good feeling only lasted for so long before the universe threw some bullshit into the air.

That was just the way life goes.

~   ~   ~

Teddy was grinning from ear to ear as the 2023 Ford Mustang Dark Horse turned onto Key Street enroute to Cody's house. His big brother, Money Mel, passed him the blunt in rotation, as they bobbed their heads to some trap music which poured from the car's impressive sound system. Teddy knew his friend would be glad to see him after what went down the night before.

Last night, when the hit on Big Boi occurred, come to find out, it was Teddy's cousin who had led the mission. His name was Bizkit. He was Teddy's Uncle Randy's son, and it was because of Bizkit that Teddy and Cody were still breathing today.

Several days ago, Mad Rodgers, a local bass player in the streets of Quincy, approached Lil Earl, who was Bizkit's righthand man, with the proposition to kill Big Boi. It was told that Big Boi and Mad had had a falling out over some old business they had conducted together. Big Boi made it clear that he wasn't budging and that if Mad wanted him to move then he would have to get it in blood. So, Mad put up twenty thousand to have the old gangster taken out, and now, Big Boi was no longer a problem.

A wild coincidence that Teddy chose to deal with Big Boi on the same night he was murdered by his cousin and his crew.

Teddy kicked himself in the ass after having placed Cody in such danger.

He promised himself to never do that again.

But little did he know, something in Cody had already awakened, and not even Cody knew of its existence, but when time permitted, he would come face to face with that inner being that sat just beyond the shadows.

When the Mustang finally arrived outside of Cody's house, Teddy spotted several vehicles parked out front that he recognized.

"Looks like the party don' already started," Money Mel said as he parked behind a burgundy Hyundai. There were four other cars present, with his being of a more luxurious model.

"Not until we're up in that bitch," added Teddy. He had bought Cody a present that he knew, without a shadow of a doubt, he would be elated to receive.

Money Mel looked at his Presidential Rolex and said, "Let's make this quick, lil bro. I gotta get on the road to Duval by noon."

"It's not like you really gotta go though, brah."

"I don't," said Money Mel.

"Then why waste your time?"

"Because he's still our old man, and he's dying, Teddy. Whether you care or not, somebody gotta be there for him. I'm just doing what needs to be done," said Money Mel.

"Then do you." Teddy reached in the back for the gift bag and got out of the car without saying another word to his brother. Just the thought of Money Mel going to visit the man who mistreated them both growing up and broke their mother's heart made him sick to his stomach. If it was up to Teddy, he would rather put a bullet in Timothy Anderson's head and be done with him.

His hatred for his father was raw.

Teddy had no love for the man who used to beat him and verbally abuse him until he felt helplessly broken.

He hated Money Mel for even caring.

Before Teddy could reach the doorstep, it opened, and there stood Avery and Ava, the twins. They were seventeen and a very complicated pair to deal with.

"It's about time you showed up, Teddy!" Ava replied, reaching out for his hand and pulling him into the house. "Cody is not happy right now."

"What's wrong wit' him?"

"Worried about your ugly ass," she said.

"I'm good," said Teddy.

When the twins and Teddy entered the noisy living room, Cody's head shoot up from where he was sitting in front of the large flatscreen Sony TV with an Xbox game controller in his hand. When he saw his friend, Cody jumped to his feet and rushed over to where Tami had intercepted Teddy to relieve him of the gift bag he was carrying.

"What's up, birthday boy!?" said Teddy with a grin, as he and Cody dapped each other up with a brotherly hug. "You good?"

"I am now," said Cody. Then, he leaned in closer where only Teddy could hear what he had to say. "I was worried about you, fat boy. I'm sorry I left you like that last night."

"That ain't about nothin', brah. We good. Happy birthday, my nigga!" Teddy grinned broadly, and that was all Cody needed to hear to give his heart peace.

Then, Money Mel entered the house with two bottles of champagne and a brand-new G-Shock watch and fitted cap for Cody. From that moment on, all the way until noon, they hung out, laughed, and just enjoyed one another's company.

And then, Cody surprised them all (his crew) when he wanted to celebrate with a nice fat blunt.

"Not before you see what I bought you for your birthday, brah," Teddy told him.

"That's right," said Cody. "You did bring something in with you earlier. What was it?" He wanted to know, and Teddy beckoned Cody to follow him.

Cody, already sporting his new G-Shock and fitted cap, followed his closest friend down the hall to his bedroom. When the door opened, to their surprise, Tami was occupying the room. And she was standing over her son's bed, stuffing something down inside her bra. At the sound of the door opening, Tami turned around, startled, looking like a deer caught in the headlights.

"Mama, what're you doing?" asked Cody.

"Nothing," she answered too quickly.

Teddy frowned and said, "I knew I couldn't trust you to keep it real, Mama Tee."

Cody looked at him in astonishment. "What's going on, Teddy?" he asked.

With a stern look on his face, Teddy told him that the gift bag not only contained a pair of Gucci sunglasses but the money he was asking for in exchange for the half ounce of molly he had. Teddy had managed to sell the half ounce to Bizkit, and there Tami was, trying to steal some of the money.

When Cody turned his gaze on his mother, she tried to give him that dark scowl that worked on him so many times before. But this time, it didn't faze him. Cody walked right up to her, took the gift bag away from her possession, extracted the sunglasses and put them on, then turned his back on his mother and made his exit without a backwards glance.

Tami couldn't even say anything because she knew that what she did was dead wrong.

But Cody refused to allow her actions to ruin his day. He had a game plan. This was his moment, one that he didn't even know he was ready for.

Chapter 5

And that moment came sometime later that evening while Cody and his crew were hanging out at the rec center downtown.

Him, the twins, and Teddy were still in their party groove after having smoked their fifth blunt of Girl Scout Cookie. A community basketball game was in session, and the crew was up in the bleachers, munching on junk food and clowning. Then, Tink Tink walked into the building, followed by her best friend/cousin, Breanna, and that was all Teddy needed to see to elevate his spirits.

He was a fool for her smile and those soft, hazel brown eyes.

"There goes my baby," Teddy sang as he stood up and began descending the steps down to the platform where he intended to make his way toward Tink Tink.

Ava shook her head amusingly. "Just like a nigga," she said with a shrug. "When pussy is around, you forget about what matters the most."

"The team," Cody replied.

"Right."

"But I don't blame Teddy though. I like Tink Tink. She's cool peoples," said Avery.

"Yeah." Ava glanced over at her twin. "She's cool until she can't have her way."

"Sounds like somebody else we know, huh, Avery?" Cody handed his friend the bag of chili cheese Fritos he was in the process of fucking up.

Avery smirked at his twin sister and said, "Sounds exactly like somebody we know."

That was when Ava mushed him in the head. Although she was the only girl in the crew, the fellas treated Ava equally. She was more of a tomboy than anything and one helluva wide receiver when you needed one. She considered herself one of the guys, and at every turn, her brothers made it their business to toughen her up.

While they perched on the bleachers, laid back, chillin', the crew watched as Teddy made his way over to where Tink Tink stood alongside her friend.

"I'm surprised Tink Tink's outside right now after what happened to her uncle last night."

"I don't see why she shouldn't," said Ava. "It didn't have nothing to do wit' her."

Avery said, "How do you know, fat mouth?"

"I'm just saying, Twin. What could Tink possibly have done to get her uncle killed?"

No sooner than the words left Ava's mouth did Cody see Tink Tink lunge herself at Teddy. Then, his eyes caught the gleam of something in Tink Tink's hand just before she swung it at Teddy again.

"Oh, shit! Teddy!" Ava was up on her feet and rushing toward Teddy at once. Both Cody and Avery followed suit and were bounding down the bleachers in a panic to reach their brother.

By this time, Tink Tink was twisting her fist into Teddy's shirt for a tighter grip and was swinging what appeared to be a blade at his face and body mass.

There was blood everywhere.

Teddy was so desperate to get away that he managed to slip himself out of the shirt he was wearing. But by this time, the damage was already done.

That still didn't stop Ava from tackling Tink Tink to the floor and attempting to beat her face in. Then, Breanna intervened by kicking Ava in the head. Avery hit her so hard that he sent her sliding across the bloody floor. Then, he pounced on Tink Tink along with his twin, and together, they gave her a vicious thrashing.

When Cody made it to Teddy, he was shocked to see his friend's face was slashed gruesomely, giving him a mask of horror and fright as he stumbled about blindly in his terror.

Suddenly, total chaos erupted around them as help came, and the violent interactions were brought to a halt. Then, the ambulance showed up, along with the police, and Teddy was rushed to the hospital immediately. And so was Tink Tink, who the twins had beaten into unconsciousness before being restrained and held until the authorities arrived. Both Avery and his sister were cuffed and led away into the back of a police cruiser.

To Cody's dismay, he wasn't implicated in the violent incident, but he did watch as his friends were taken away from him in opposite directions.

He was left alone to fend for himself.

"This is crazy," Cody muttered to himself as he stood outside the rec center, watching Teddy get driven away in an ambulance.

Today didn't even feel like a birthday anymore.

"Shit!" Cody glanced down at his Jordans and saw that they were splashed with blood.

Teddy's blood.

"Sonavabitch!" he bellowed. Cody could only shake his head and curse his luck. "Fuck these punk ass shoes!" he snapped and slunk away in absolute distress.

~   ~   ~

Jada was snapping her fingers and dancing in her seat, as she pushed her Subaru WRX Limited down Pat Thomas

Road on her way home. She had just gotten back in town from her business excursion over in Tallahassee. Her nail shop would be up and running soon, and Jada couldn't wait to finally bring her dream to light.

Singing along to Ella Mai crooning from her digital stereo system, Jada stopped in mid-vocal when her headlights spotted a familiar face walking alongside the highway by himself. Jada didn't even waste time considering what she would do next. She hit her blinkers and bent a right turn along a side street. She then pushed her Subaru around the backside of the block, swung around right behind the old police station, then hopped back on Pat Thomas where she was now coming up behind her person of interest. Jada honked the horn once before sliding the Subaru aside to bring herself alongside of him walking down the street.

"Cody," she called out to him as she brought the vehicle ahead of his path. "Cody!"

Cody looked up and saw Jada staring at him through her side window. "What's going on, Jada?"

"What are you doing out here? Get in," Jada told him before reaching over to push the passenger door open, so he could climb inside.

Cody got inside without being told twice.

"I got blood on my clothes," he warned her.

"What!?" Jada gasped, and the car jerked violently.

He sighed miserably and told her what had just went down back at the rec center.

"Damn. So, where were you headed just now?" Jada wanted to know.

"To the hospital," he said.

"You was about to walk all the way to the hospital, Cody? I find that hard to believe. Why didn't you just go along with Teddy in the ambulance?"

"Too much was going on," he said humbly. Cody wanted so badly to tell her what was really on his mind, but he didn't want her to panic.

"Okay, I'll take you to the hospital," said Jada. "Then, I'm gonna call Tami to come…"

"No."

"No?" Jada glanced at him.

"Me and Mama ain't seeing eye to eye right now."

"Oh. What happened?" she asked. "What did Tami do?"

"Stole from me."

What Cody didn't expect to hear was her laughter, but she cut it short to refocus on the seriousness of the matter. "That's trifling as hell," she said.

Jada and Tami were working partners over at Divas' Palace Hair Salon before everything went to shits for Tami. Some items had been stolen from the salon and come to find out, Tami was the culprit. She had stolen over two thousand dollars' worth of materials, only to barter it all out for money to support her molly habit. So, it wasn't a surprise to Jada that her old work partner was still up to her old tricks.

"Okay, Cody. I won't call her," she replied, heading toward Quincy Hospital. "But don't expect for me to do more than what I should be doing. I'm only giving you a ride, baby."

"That's all I want," Cody said. "I can handle the rest when I get there."

Chapter 6

Shequita Daniels stormed through the hospital entrance with Money Mel long-striding alongside of her. When she got the call about Teddy being hurt and rushed to the hospital, she abandoned her duties working at the local senior citizen home out in East Quincy. She hopped in her car and floored it all the way to the hospital. Then, it so happened that Money Mel was pulling up just as she angled her Dodge Magnum into the hospital's service entrance. He had just made it back in town when his baby mama's sister, Brandi, who worked at the hospital as a licensed practical nurse, called to inform Money Mel of his baby brother's status.

Now, mother and son entered the building like a pair of hyenas, ready to tear some shit up about Teddy. He was the baby of their family. And for Teddy, they both would go to the ends of the earth to be there for him.

Money Mel hated himself for leaving Teddy the way he had earlier, but Teddy didn't understand that regardless of how cruel their father was to them, Timothy Anderson had once been a great man.

He wasn't always a bad father.

The man had mental issues he was dealing with the only way he knew how.

Let Teddy tell it, he was his own father; he made himself who he was today. And he blamed their mother for not being brave enough to stand up against his father all those years, succumbing to his abuse. That was why Teddy stabbed him with that butcher knife that night when he was just eight years old. All he had to see was his father slapping his mother around to take matters in his own hands.

Teddy was a fearless little creature.

He was loyal.

Prior to reaching the hospital, Money Mel asked Brandi to be waiting in the lobby for him, so he wouldn't have to go through the motions with the lobbyist. And that was exactly where she was when him and his mother stormed through the doors. Brandi McNeil was standing next to the information desk, conferring with one of her colleagues.

"Where is my brotha?" Money Mel demanded the instant he reached the desk. "Is he okay?"

Brandi was of a walnut brown skin complexion, too heavy but very curvaceous. She stood just an inch shorter than Shequita, but the older woman's physique was more pronounced due to normal exercise activities at work.

"Teddy just came outta surgery and was taken to his assigned room in the ICU," said Brandi, looking damn good in her pink and blue scrubs.

That was when Shequita spoke up. "I need to see my baby."

"I'll take you to him," she said.

Brandi shot a knowing glance in Money Mel's direction, then she placed a gentle hand upon the mother's back and guided her to Teddy's room.

"His friend's in there wit' him," said Brandi.

"What friend? I'm told his friends all got arrested back at the rec center." Shequita explained what she had learned from a friend of a friend who was present in the building that evening. Emmanuel Thomas was one of the players on the basketball court who rushed to break up the commotion.

"Cody's wit' him, Ms. Quita," Brandi said.

"Cody," Teddy's mother sighed. Then, she wondered why he hadn't called her himself to tell her about what had gone down tonight.

Shequita sped up her pace to reach the room so that she could interrogate Cody herself. But once she stepped foot inside the room and saw Cody dressed with Teddy's blood on his clothing, she rushed to him with open arms.

Just several hours ago, she was wishing him a happy birthday. Now there she was, wishing she could have prevented what she saw in Cody's eyes.

The boy looked deranged.

He was saddened.

Money Mel saw it too, but he couldn't say that he came to the same conclusion as his mother. There was something else he saw in Cody at the moment, something dark and waiting to be set free.

He saw that beast in him.

"Tell me what happened to my baby, Cody." Shequita sounded almost like she was pleading with him. She was a tough woman, but that happened when you'd experienced the hell her life had been through.

Cody had to sit down to tell her everything. He told her about the molly, but not who gave it to him, then about Teddy suggesting that Big Boi would buy it. When Shequita heard this part, she shifted uneasily in her seat beside him. Then, he went on to tell her about what he did back at the rec center.

"I didn't care about nothing else," he said. "I just wanted to make sure my brotha was alright."

Money Mel nodded his head understandably and gazed over at Teddy's bed. His baby brother had been cut and stabbed multiple times. There were bandages all over his face and body that the surgical team applied to his wounds.

Eyes welling up with tears, Shequita took Cody's hand and squeezed it reassuringly. "Thank you for being there for my baby," she softly replied.

"That's my brotha," he said.

"So, for Tink Tink to do what she did, somebody had to tell her that y'all was there last night," Money Mel finally spoke up.

Cody said nothing. He had come to the same conclusion as Money Mel.

"I'll find out," said Money Mel.

"You better do something." Shequita looked up at her son and said. "Look at my baby! He could've been killed tonight." She then stood up and approached Teddy's bed and touched his arm gently. "Somebody needs to pay for this," she muttered. "They must pay tonight."

That was all Money Mel needed to hear. He nodded his head at his mother's turned back. Then, he made his way to the door without saying another word.

Cody watched him go in grave silence.

The pressure was up now, and the intensity of it left you wondering what would happen next.

There was blood in the air.

Teddy's blood.

And tonight, somebody else was about to die.

~   ~   ~

During the same hour, Treyvon Conyers, aka Trey, was putting flame to his Black&Mild cigar while sitting in the passenger seat of a dark colored Chevy Tahoe. In his mind, all he could think about was the images of finding his father dead in the living room of his house last night. Trey, at twenty-three years old, had never seen anything so wicked in his life.

No son should see some shit like that.

But he couldn't shake the images, which only made the beast in him want to scream.

"There he go right there," said Blue, pointing out his side window at Money Mel exiting the hospital. Trey reached for the Tec-9 resting in his lap. He wasn't stupid. He knew this was the wrong place to pop off, so he forced himself to remain steadfast.

"I see him, brah," Trey replied.

"And there's the police too so just chill."

Trey saw them too. A QPD cruiser had arrived on the scene minutes ago and parked next to the ER entrance building. There were two cops inside, but one of them went inside while the other stayed behind. He was still sitting inside the car with its passenger door wide open. It appeared as though he was on the radio with the dispatcher or somebody.

Money Mel was headed for his truck near the east end of the hospital's parking lot.

Moments after he made his exit, the entrance door opened and out came Cody. He called out to Money Mel's retreating figure. He stopped and turned toward the voice, and Cody rushed over to him.

"That must be the other little nigga too, huh?" Blue shifted in his seat anxiously. He wasn't originally from Pepper Hill like Trey and the others. Blue lived out in Mount Pleasant all his life, but he eventually made Shaw Quarters his second home.

Trey didn't respond. He smoked his cigar and watched as Cody and Money Mel stood there, conversing. Between the both of them, their interactions were sharpened by aggravation and heartfelt emotion. Trey could only guess what their heated conversation was about.

It was war time, and Trey wanted blood — more blood to be exact. Because last night, after finding out that Sugar Foot was with Big Boi just before he died, he sought and found her, and then he murdered her in cold blood. But not before torturing information out of her first, which brought him to this point. After learning about Cody and Teddy's involvement, Trey called his Uncle Lenny, who was Tink Tink's father, and informed on what he learned. Unfortunately, Tink Tink must have been around when he shared the information with her father last night because how else would she know who to target at the rec center that evening? Apparently, she had conducted her own investigation on the matter and took matters into her own hands.

Tink Tink had made Trey proud tonight, despite the fact that she had been moving wrong and reckless. Now, she was lying in that same hospital with a concussion after being jumped by the twins. And that was a whole other situation in itself.

Her honor wasn't going unavenged either.

This whole situation was messed up, and no one was safe as long as she was hurting.

After their heated exchange, Money Mel and Cody made their way to the Mustang and got in.

"Let's get it, baby." Blue started up the Tahoe in anticipation, and Trey finally curved his finger around the trigger of his weapon.

Blue waited until the car pulled out into traffic before he made a move to follow. The Mustang was headed back toward town, and Blue never let it leave his sight.

Chapter 7

The only reason why they hadn't seen Money Mel's car leave was because Wesley had taken the rear entrance of the hospital on the other side. Next to him, in the front seat, was Tami, rocking back-and-forth anxiously to get to her son.

Also occupying the car was Felicia Bradwell, Avery and Ava's mother. It was her who had phoned Tami about the rec center incident. Both of her children were being processed at the Department of Juvenile Justice center for assault and battery. That was crazy when all the twins did was go to Teddy's rescue against an armed individual. It wasn't like they had initiated the whole incident. But Felicia would deal with that matter later. It was too late to rescue her children now. By morning, they would be assigned to the juvenile detention center, and there was not a damn thing she could do about that.

But she could be there for her friends, Tami and Shequita. They all had come up together in the same hood and in the same circle. Their loyalties were etched in stone, and tonight would prove that belief.

When the car pulled up outside the entrance door of the hospital, Tami wasted no time opening her door and demanding Wesley to let her out there.

"Me too," said Felicia, opening her door in the back and getting out along with her friend.

"I'll be right in," Wesley replied. "Let me find a parkin' spot right quick."

Tami and Felicia were already headed for the front door entrance of the hospital. They already knew which room Teddy was assigned to and headed straight there.

Minutes later, Felicia was the first to enter the room with Tami on her heels. But what they found inside was something totally unexpected. Shequita was tussling with another woman as one tried to get the best of the other. They were choking one another, grabbing each other's hair, clawing and cursing up a storm.

Tami sprang into action at once and grabbed ahold of the other woman. She held her while Shequita got herself in a few solid licks before she started screaming at the top of her lungs.

Felicia punched her dead in the mouth. "Shut the fuck up, bitch!"

By this time, the room door swung open, and there stood Raymond Williams, a homicide detective for Quincy Police Department. He had shown up just in time before Tami started dropping some mean blows on the woman.

"Break this mess up! Right now! Stop!" Detective Raymond Williams pointed a stern finger at Tami, who looked like she wanted to test his patience. "Don't make me slap some cuffs on you, Tami."

"You don't have to do all that." Wesley walked through the door next, his big, stocky frame filling up the already crowded room.

"Good. Now straighten your woman, Wes," said the detective, unquestionably familiar with pretty much everybody in the room. Then, he stepped forward to help the other woman up off the floor. "What're you doing in here, Jill? Aren't you supposed to be watching over your daughter right now?" he chastised her.

Jill Davis looked up at the tall detective with scorn written all over her face. This was Tink Tink's mother, the wife of Lenny Davis, and the way things looked, it appeared that Jill had come to confront Shequita about what went down tonight with their children.

And that was exactly what Jill explained to Raymond, as if her actions were justifiable enough to win his vote of understanding.

"You're playing a dangerous game, Jill. Please return back to your daughter's room. I'll be there to finish talkin' to you next," said Detective Williams.

"This shit ain't over, Quita. Just so that you know," Jill said over her shoulder as she was being escorted to the door by the detective.

"Don't," Wesley said to Shequita, who looked like she was about to go back after the woman. "Calm down and clean yourself up," he hissed.

With that being said, Felicia rushed over to the bathroom to get something to help her friend clean herself up with.

"That bitch gon' make me kill her about my baby," Shequita replied venomously.

"Be very careful what you say, Shequita," warned Detective Williams after seeing Jill out the door.

"Why are you even here, Ray?" Tami asked.

"To talk to your son."

"About what?" said Felicia.

"About this," said the detective, materializing with a clear evidence bag containing what appeared to be a LA Lakers ballcap.

When Tami saw the snapback ballcap, her heart began to race with sudden dread.

"Found this at the scene of Big Boi's murder," said Detective Williams. "It was in the hallway leading to the opened back door on the floor."

"That hat could belong to anybody," said Wesley.

"Not when Cody's signature is inscribed beneath the bill, marking it as being his property." When Raymond said this, both Wesley and Tami looked at each other in cold, silent fear for Cody.

He had a habit of putting his name on everything he considered his, and the snapback indeed belonged to him.

Now Tami was really scared for her son.

The shit had just gotten real.

~   ~   ~

Cody had convinced Money Mel that he was up for whatever it was that he had in mind to seek vengeance against those who opposed against them.

Cody told him straight up that if he didn't bring him along then he would find his own way. Not wanting to waste time arguing with Cody, and not wanting anything to happen to him either, Money Mel agreed to bring him along for this gangsta ride.

It was a murder mission.

While Cody wallowed in his thoughts on what was about to transpire, Money Mel was on the phone with Bizkit.

They were discussing the matter at hand and making plans to meet up. Bizkit was out in the New Projects across town, laying low with his side chick.

"Well, it's up right now, cuz. Link up wit' me later after you finish doing what you doing."

"I'm 'bout to roll out in a minute anyway," said Bizkit, smashing what was left of his plate of food that Niecy had cooked for him. "And you say you got lil' Cody wit' you too, cuz?"

Money Mel glanced over to his right. "Yeah."

"Bad move, Mel."

"The nigga left me wit' no other choice, cuz."

"There's always a choice," said Bizkit. "But don't sweat it, my nigga. We gon' make it do what it do. Just make sure you watch your back out there."

"Always."

"You know them clowns lurkin'." Bizkit was referring to Trey and whoever was riding with him. Trey was smart and ruthless, like his father had been, so there was no sleeping on him.

Money Mel ended the call with the assurance that he was very much on point. Then, he checked his rearview mirror and saw that the SUV that had left the hospital not long after him was managing to keep a discreet distance behind the Mustang. But Money Mel was not moved by this distraction for he had done this same thing many times before.

To catch him slippin' one would really have to be swifter than whoever was occupying the truck riding behind him at the moment.

"Cody," Money Mel broke the silence between them.

Cody looked over at him. "What's up, Mel?"

"I want you to recline your seat as far back as it would go. That way, when it's time to move, I want you to slide in the back and lay low."

"What's going on, Mel?"

"Somebody is following us, and I just wanna make sure you straight, lil brah."

When Cody made a move to look behind him, Money Mel stilled him with a solid hand to the chest. He told Cody to never look back because looking back would alert the enemy that you were on to them.

"And then there's no tellin' how the tables will turn after that," said Money Mel.

Cody did as he was told. "Who do you think it is?" he asked.

"None of that matters right now, Cody. Whoever it is don't mean us no good." Money Mel hit the blinkers once he passed the old Sacks Grocery, then he turned left onto Stewart Street. Eyes still on his rearview mirror, Money Mel reached beneath his seat for the .44 Magnum he had there.

At the sight of the gun, Cody knew without a shadow of a doubt it was about to go down.

The Mustang sped down Stewart Street and slowed down to make another turn on a side street. Once he made the turn,

Money Mel stomped on the brakes, threw the car in park, and hopped out with his gun cocked and ready.

The dark colored Tahoe was making its way up the street, and Money Mel laid in wait for the right moment to take action.

Then, the unexpected happened. The Chevy Tahoe came to a complete stop in the middle of the street about forty yards away from where Money Mel stood.

Nobody moved for a long moment.

For some reason, the truck refused to fall for the bait. Whoever was inside knew something was up and was avoiding the inevitable.

It didn't take Money Mel long to realize what was going on and step out from the shadows into the street. He stood ten toes down right there in the middle of Stewart Street in the sights of the Tahoe's headlights.

"What's up? What you niggas wanna do?!" Money Mel threw his arms up in a challenging gesture.

Moments later, a body protruded from the passenger window, carrying what looked like an assault rifle. Then, the Tahoe shot forward as automatic rounds rang out from the gunman hanging out the window.

Money Mel let his .44 Magnum roar as he stood his ground, but he moved swiftly along the street as he sent rounds back at the SUV.

This was cause for Cody to look back, and when he did, he saw Money Mel's body jerk violently and slump to the ground. This freaked Cody out, and instead of doing what Money Mel demanded of him, he slid behind the wheel of the car.

The Tahoe continued up the street and brought itself to a halt alongside Money Mel's fallen body lying next to the curb. This put Money Mel and the driver on the same side of the street. Then, just when Cody thought it was over, Money Mel sprang to his feet with his cannon blazing.

"Oh, shit!" Cody watched in astonishment as Money Mel gunned down the driver and rushed the SUV fast, so as not to allow the gunman to get a shot off at him.

Nine shots later, Money Mel was hurrying back to the Mustang and snatched the driver door open. When he saw Cody sitting behind the wheel, he frowned and said, "Nigga, I ain't dead yet! Scoot your ass back over to the other side."

"I thought you was dead," said Cody.

"Nah," said Money Mel with a grin. "I was just playing possum wit' them fools. Checkmate," he added as he took his rightful place behind the wheel.

Chapter 8

Alisha was in the process of pulling her car up in the driveway of her house when she noticed someone standing on the front porch of Tami's house.

As she was exiting her car with her bags in one hand and the other hand jabbed down into her purse where her .380 pistol was, Alisha watched the man remove himself from the porch.

"Hey, Alisha," the voice called out to her, and she instantly recognized it.

"Corey?" she answered, no longer suspicious but now weary of his presence. This was Cody's biological father, the heavy gambler and two-time felon who Tami once loved and cherished years ago. But that was before his gambling sickness brought trouble to their front door, and Tami was subjected to being assaulted because of it. That was ten years ago, and Tami still wore the scars from that fateful day in her own foyer.

And then, Corey hunted them suckers down and killed every last one of them. Then, he was sent off to prison to do a six-year bid for violent offenses. He got out for a year and some change and went back to prison over some bullshit. He'd been home now for eleven months, trying to do the right thing, but still could not find a stable job. Tami didn't want anything to do with him, but for the sake of the son they shared, she had no choice but to deal with him.

Cody didn't see his father much, and he pretty much didn't care to. Though they spoke often whenever Corey found the time to stop by or whenever he happened to bump into him in the streets.

But Cody wasn't like Teddy. He acknowledged his father and gave him the benefit of the doubt. Overall, he knew Corey existed, but he would rather Corey focused more on himself than missed opportunities with him.

"My son's in trouble, and I stopped by to see if I can help out somehow," said Corey.

"What do you mean Cody's in trouble?" Alisha asked curiously, wondering if this was some type of bullshit excuse that Corey had cooked up.

"He's in serious trouble."

"How so?"

Corey cut across the front yard to where Alisha was standing two feet away from her own doorstep. "Got a call from my old partna, Ray, about my son being involved in a murder last night."

"A murder? Really, Corey?!" Alisha looked at the man like he'd lost his damn mind. "I highly doubt that Cody has the heart to kill anybody."

"Maybe it wasn't him that actually killed Big Boi," said Corey.

At the mention of the name, Alisha froze. She had heard all about the murder of Big Boi. He was a street legend and former star athlete whose dreams went down the drain at the snap of a finger.

Thinking about Big Boi made Alisha think about Trey and what he could possibly be going through. She liked Trey, but he was too wild for her taste. And it made her very uncomfortable to hear that Cody had been implicated in the murder of Trey's father. Now all it took was for Trey to hear it and set his sights on Cody and do something very drastic.

So, yeah, thought Alisha, *Corey has a right to be worried about his son.*

"That's bad, Corey. Where is Tami?" she asked.

"Your guess is as good as mines, Alisha. But if I was a betting man, I'd say she's with that boyfriend of hers," he replied.

"But you are a betting man," she retorted.

He just shrugged in response.

"Well, if you do find your son, maybe that's the time where you really should step up to the plate. But go get to it, Corey. Stay safe. Okay?"

Corey nodded. "That's mandatory."

She didn't respond. She opened her front door and let herself inside. Once inside, Alisha put her bags away onto the kitchen counter and then retrieved her cell phone to call her brother.

"Did you get the package?" Twan answered after two rings.

"That's not why I'm calling, Antwan," she said.

Pause.

Then, Twan said, "Why are you callin' then?" His tone was laden with suspicion.

"I need a serious favor from you, Twan."

"Okay." He waited to hear more.

"It's about my boo, Cody, from next door."

"My little hustle man," said Twan.

Alisha shook her head. "Well, your little hustle man is wanted for murder, and I need you to work your magic to save him if you can."

"Wanted for murder? Who?"

"Big Boi," she said.

A long breath was released from the other end of the phone. "That's not good, sis."

"My point exactly."

"Trey?" Twan only had to say that one name.

Alisha then closed her eyes. "I wish it wasn't but yes, Antwan. And you know why I need for you to stop this before it happens."

Because it wouldn't be the first time Trey killed a kid. He had done it once before, and Alisha had been standing just a foot away. It was almost like she could still smell the blood as it splattered from TJ's brain onto her face.

That had happened a long time ago. Her and Trey were just sixteen at the time, and TJ was only an innocent fifteen-year-old kid.

Trey had killed TJ over Alisha because he thought he liked her too much. And still till this day, Alisha couldn't figure out what TJ did to make Trey shoot him that morning.

But she never said a word about it, only that the killer wore a mask. But Twan knew what really happened.

If only she had told the truth.

There would be no Trey Conyers.

And Cody would at least have a fighting chance than having to deal with that kind of monster.

~   ~   ~

And speaking of which, after Shequita explained to Tami what happened with Cody and why he left with her oldest son, Tami turned her pleading gaze on the man in her life. She needed not to tell Wesley what he should be doing. He nodded his head solemnly and hurried off to go look for Cody.

Meanwhile, Detective Raymond Williams was rectifying the mothers of the severity of the matter. That no one would come out of this clean or unaffected. That too much blood had been spilled already, including that of young Sugar Foot, who was discovered beaten to death with a blunt object in a back room of a local crack house. At hearing this, Felicia reached for her phone to call Margarette Shorter, her dear friend and Sugar Foot's godmother.

"And it's not gonna stop there if we don't round up those we need to locate and determine who's the actual murderer," said Ray.

"So, you don't believe my son is the one?" Tami heard herself ask the detective before she even realized that she'd spoken out loud.

"Yes," he said. "But I'm pretty sure that your son knows who the killer is."

"Which means you intend for him to snitch?" said Shequita.

"Which will put him further at risk," Tami added and shot the man a vicious look. "To use my son as a pawn to get what you want, Ray, will get you in a serious situation with me."

The man opened his mouth to respond but was interrupted by the ringing of his cell phone. While still holding Tami's gaze, he reached to retrieve his phone and glanced down to see who was calling.

It was his boss calling. Detective Williams answered the call immediately while bolting to his feet so that he could talk more privately away from the others in the room.

Tami watched him like a hawk.

"Yes, sir. Okay, Chief. I'll get right on it, Chief," said Ray in a rush of words a minute later. Then, he ended the call and turned his gaze back on the three women before him.

"Why you looking like that, Ray?"

He looked directly at Shequita to answer her question without raising a ruckus. "There's been another shootin' just now. Over on Stewart Street. I gotta go check it out," he said.

"Didn't they say who?" asked Tami.

"No one knows anything right now, Tami. I have to go investigate for myself. I'll let you know when I know," he said.

"You'll do that for me?" Tami asked.

"Why wouldn't I?" Ray held her gaze for a moment longer then turned away and hurried out of the door. Then, just before the door could shut all the way, it opened back up, and in walked Lisa and her son, Meechie.

Seeing her sister perked Shequita up a little bit. Lisa entered the room and hurried right over to Teddy's bedside.

Shaking her head sadly, Lisa then looked up at her little sister with emotion shining in her eyes.

"It would be a dumb question to ask how he's doing when it's already clear," said Lisa, big boned and pretty as a kiss. This was the unpredictable sister, lively and always full of herself.

"Teddy's a soldier," said Shequita.

"Of course." Lisa stepped over and wrapped an arm around her sister's waist. "It's crazy out there," Lisa sighed deeply. "Big Boi is dead, and Sugar Foot, Blue from Shaw Quarters, and just now, they was rushing Trey through the doors as I was walkin' in. Somebody shot him all up, and it don't look like he's gonna pull through," she replied emotionally.

The news sparked something in Shequita that made her turn and wrap both her arms around Lisa. She knew Trey had meant a great deal to her, regardless of the differences her and Big Boi went through. Trey had always respected her, and Lisa would go out of her way to assure him of her love and loyalty.

Trey was like a son to her.

He was real.

"Have you heard from Cody yet?" Lisa asked Tami, her heart burning with grief.

Across the room, Meechie shifted uneasily as he watched his mother go through the motions. He was seventeen, smart, a good kid; Meechie was nothing like Teddy and all those he surrounded himself with.

Tami shared what she knew of her son's situation, and Lisa's mouth dropped in shock.

"I don't believe that for one second," Lisa said with another heavy sigh.

"Wes is out there lookin' for him now."

Felicia said, "Y'all won't believe what I am lookin' at right now on Facebook." In her hand was her iPhone, and that same hand was shaking nervously.

"What?" Shequita replied.

When the phone was turned toward them so they could see the screen, Tami was the first to curse, then Lisa said something unintelligible, and Shequita only just dropped her head in pure agony.

What they all were now witnessing was a reality that would live in their hearts forever. And that reality was that of Randy Griffen, who died in a gun battle tonight after killing two others. The two men he shot to death were Trey's homeboys after receiving a tip saying that they had something to do with Sugar Foot's death.

A lone tear escaped Lisa's eyes. Not only had she lost a niece tonight but a big brother too.

And Shequita was torn to pieces.

She was devastated.

Chapter 9

"That shit won't happen again," said Money Mel. He was tugging the bulletproof vest down over Cody's body and strapped it down around him tightly.

After the murder mission back over in Pepper Hill about thirty minutes ago, Money Mel headed out to his place over in Joy Land. Bizkit said he was on the way, him and the rest of the crew.

"You ever got shot wit' one of these on?" Cody asked as he shrugged his body around the vest he was wearing.

"Twice," said Money Mel.

"Did it hurt?"

He nodded. "Hurt like a muthafucker."

"But it saved your life though. I guess that's what matters the most. I'd rather deal wit' the pain than actually having a bullet in me."

After he was done with Cody, having explained to him the importance of wearing a vest, Money Mel reached for the second one laying on the bed. He shrugged it on and tightened it around him.

"Now it's time to choose your strap," he said.

"My strap? You mean a gun?"

Money Mel nodded.

"Aight. Let's do it," said Cody. Money Mel then beckoned him into the kitchen where he approached the deep freezer container and dragged it out from the wall.

"If anything ever happens to me, I want you to remember all the hiding spots I've shown you already. When we're done here, I'll show you the rest." Money Mel had had a minor artillery shelf installed behind the back of the deep freezer container. There were four of them in all, and Cody was already eyeing the one that held his attention the most.

"What's this one?" Cody reached for the second one he had been given.

"That's the Ruger.9milimeter right there. Lemme show you how to handle this bad boy." Money Mel gestured for the gun, and Cody handed it over.

There was a vehicle pulling up in the driveway outside, and they moved to the front of the house.

When Money Mel saw that it was Bizkit and the others, he went to go unlock the front door. And then, his cell phone rang. The caller ID read Felicia's name and phone number.

"What's up, Felicia?" he answered as he opened the door for the crew.

"Bring me back my baby, Melvin," Tami replied, and the coldness in her tone was real. "I'm at the hospital wit' your mama and your brotha. Where is Cody?"

"He's right here."

"Put him on the phone."

With an exasperated sigh, Money Mel turned away from the door to where Cody stood in the front room, admiring his first gun. He looked up at his approach, and Money Mel extended the phone to him.

"It's your mama," he said.

Hesitantly, Cody reached for the phone and put it to his ear. "Hey, Mama, what's up?"

"Are you alright, baby boy?" Tami replied.

"No," he said simply.

A momentary pause ensued. "Look, Cody. I apologize about what I did earlier. I still got your money. I'll give it all back to you. I admit I fucked up, and I'm sorry, baby boy. But there's too much going on out there. I'm scared, and I need you here wit' me." Tami sounded royally concerned for his wellbeing.

"You got Wesley for that, Mama."

Again, Tami was reluctant to respond. "Wes is…"

"You don't need me, Mama," he cut in.

"I do!" she cried. "I do. Please, Cody, come here from out there in them streets. That's not you. You ain't no damn thug. I raised you better than that, Cody. You ain't built for that type of lifestyle. I know you're not," she said.

That was the wrong choice of words, thought Cody, and he wished he didn't have to do what he was contemplating doing.

"Cody?" she called out to him.

"Yeah, Mama."

"You heard me?" she said.

He shook his head no. "Don't worry about me, Mama. I'ma be aight. I'll talk to you later."

"No!"

But the phone was already disconnecting, and Cody could just imagine the horrified look on his mother's face. He brushed away the wicked images and turned his attention on the guys around him.

Bizkit was on real demon time as he was attired in all-black and sporting a black and grey Raiders' fitted cap. Then, there was Lil Earl, Lank, Dred, and Po'Boy from Lake Skillet. The room was filled with a team of bonafide killas, and Cody felt so out of place in their company.

"What it do, lil one?" Po'Boy was the first to acknowledge Cody and reached his meaty hand out for some dap.

Cody bumped fists with him. "Chillin."

Then, Bizkit stepped up and gave Cody a long, hard gaze. Cody dared not break eye contact, and for a brief moment, he thought the nigga was about to do something to him.

"You got away last night," said Bizkit.

Cody lifted his chin up.

"But here you stand, huh? Vest on and toting your pistol," Bizkit smirked. "I don't see it though. I don't think you got it in you."

"He got it," said Money Mel.

"We'll see," Bizkit replied. Then, he dismissed Cody like he was a nobody, which only began to play on his conscience. Cody wasn't dumb by a long shot. He knew where this was going. He knew he would be tested tonight to no ends, and Cody was really not ready, but one thing was for damn sure. He intended on making them out to be a believer.

~   ~   ~

Meanwhile, Wesley was seething mad as he ended the call with Tami. She was beside herself with worry, and now Cody had caused her to be livid. For a second, Tami had spazzed out on him, and Wesley had to check her about talking to him so disrespectfully. He loved his woman, but he was not going to allow Tami to talk to him any kind of way. He didn't care how angry and scared she was. Tami needed to tone that shit down. But he understood her concern over Cody and what she believed he was now being pressured to do. All his friends were gone or hurt, leaving him out there to fend for himself, so now he felt he had something to prove regarding where his loyalty was concerned.

And that was what Wesley was afraid of, Cody stepping into a lifestyle that wasn't fit for him.

Cody was not that tough.

He was confused.

Wesley had been a part of his stepson's life long enough to know how he was feeling. He knew Cody didn't think too kindly of him at times, all because of his mother's molly habit. He knew Cody blamed him for all the missed opportunities and special moments he felt he didn't have with his mother anymore — all because of her molly habits.

Ever since Tami started consuming molly, everything seemed like it was going downhill for Cody. His mother had changed, and with that change came a dire need for Cody to want the old Tami back.

But it wasn't Wesley's fault; it was Tami who had initiated their arrangement. She was poppin' molly way before he came into the picture.

But you couldn't tell Cody that though. He just needed somebody else to blame rather than his mother.

In his heart of hearts, Wesley truly cared for the boy. He wanted something special with Cody — that special connection where a son looked up to his father and knew in his heart that he was in the right hands. He wanted what was best for Cody. That was why he bought him the new Xbox game system for his birthday. Wesley was a gamer himself and doing this for Cody created a special something between them. He prided himself on being able to peel away at least a little bit of that shield of protection he had around him.

What was going on now was a whole other ball game that Wesley didn't see coming. Now he had to race to find Cody before he did something stupid. Losing Cody to the streets was one thing, but losing the innocence that was in him was another.

The gas light alerted Wesley that he needed to refuel, so he searched for the nearest station.

Minutes later, he was pulling the car through the entrance of a Golden Falcon gas station and brought it to a halt next to a service pump. He got out and preceded to refuel his car.

Another car suddenly parked across from his at another pump. But it was who Wesley saw exit the car that made him brace himself with caution.

"Just the person I needed to see," said Corey, stepping between the twin gas pumps to face Wesley.

"How's it going, Corey?"

The other man frowned. "Like a goddamn nightmare," he said, and Wesley couldn't agree with him more.

Chapter 10

It wasn't a pissing contest. There was no animosity in the air toward one another for both men had long ago moved past that stage. But there was a sense of pride there, both men looking for the same outcome and that outcome being Cody's safety and bringing him back home unscathed.

"When's the last time you saw him?"

"At the little get together we had at the house for him earlier," Wesley answered.

"You had a birthday party for him?" Corey asked, mad that he wasn't able to make it. He had so many appointments today at the doctor's office, his PO schedule, a job interview; Corey couldn't make it if he tried.

"It was just a get together, nothing major." Then, Wesley told him about the incident that led them both out tonight looking for Cody.

This was the second person who related this story to him, and all it did was cause Corey to grow even more worried. He had spoken with Raymond Williams and Lenny Davis and gotten the full scoop on the situation.

"You heard about Randy?" said Wesley.

Corey nodded. "All the reason to find my boy and get him outta these streets," he added gravely.

"I think I know where he's at," said Wesley.

"Where?" Corey reacted.

"He's wit' Quita's son, Mel. At least that's who he ran off with earlier. But Tami said she talked to him not long ago, and Cody wasn't talking right."

"What you mean he wasn't talkin' right, Wes?"

"He's committed, Corey," he said.

Corey didn't reply.

"He feels he has something to prove by going after those who poses a threat to himself and those he love," Wesley added with a long breath.

"My car or yours?" said Corey.

"It don't even matter wit' me, man. All I want is to find Cody."

After parking his car near the shoulder of the gas station, Corey hopped in the passenger seat next to Wesley. If Tami could see them now, she would probably lose her damn mind if not already.

While Wesley drove, Corey worked his phone, trying to find a connection to Money Mel. It was clarified that Cody was in his company, and there was no telling what they both were planning to do.

~   ~   ~

When the blunt made it around to Cody, he took it and put it to his mouth. Those around him watched with anticipation, not knowing that Cody did not possess virgin lungs. He hit the blunt and inhaled then exhaled out a train of weed smoke directly in Bizkit's direction.

Lank thought it was amusing to watch Bizkit and Cody go back-and-forth, teasing one another. But he knew eventually that Bizkit was going to apply so much pressure on Cody that it would be a wonder not to see him fold.

It was only a matter of time, and Cody had better hope he had the guts to hang.

In the meantime, the crew was discussing the probabilities they were faced with regarding their mission.

The streets of Quincy were on fire with the latest shootings. So, they would have to move swiftly and with ruthlessness in order to make it out alive and without being apprehended in the process.

Their only threats now were two people, and they were Bo Ford and Lenny Davis' nephew, Tysheed, who was making too much noise about what went down with Tink Tink and now Trey. He was a young hellraiser with a growing reputation. And Bo Ford, he and Big Boi were solid partners, and it had been told he was seeking answers in the streets. These two individuals could pose a serious problem, and they needed to be dealt with accordingly.

The plan was to split up in two groups and execute their marks with precision.

"Bo is highly regarded as the more serious threat. That old nigga is militant and smart. He's been doing this shit a long time. You can't play wit' him," said Dred, the oldest in the room. He was thirty years old and ruthless as a rattlesnake. "When you see him, you gotta do him in right there."

"Sounds like you scared of that old nigga," Lil Earl smirked over at Dred.

"Naw," he said. "I just know better."

"Okay," Money Mel spoke up. "What or where is more likely we can find Bo Ford? What are his weaknesses?"

"I've never known he had a weakness for anything," said Bizkit, who used to mess around with his granddaughter, Kamillah, on the low. Her family was very strict about her dealing with street dudes, but Kamillah was of the rebellious type; she went after what she liked.

Using Kamillah was the last thing Bizkit wanted to do, and besides, she was way down in Orlando, following her dreams of being a professional photographer.

The crew had continued to discuss the importance of eliminating the threats when the sound of a vehicle pulling up outside caught their attention. Lank was the first to rise and move over to the window and peer into the darkness of night.

"Who is it, Lank?" asked Money Mel.

"Can't really tell," he replied. "But it looks like two dudes gettin' outta the car though."

At hearing this, Money Mel got up to go see for himself. When he saw who the two men were, he did a double take as they stepped upon the front porch. Then, he glanced back at Cody with a solemn look on his face.

Cody caught the look he gave him and wondered what it was that affected him so much.

And then the front door was opened, and both Wesley and Corey walked inside the house. Cody was befuddled when he laid eyes on his father and Wesley. Seeing them together caught him totally off guard.

"What's going on, fellas?" said Corey, acknowledging the crew but looking directly at his son.

"You see it, OG," said Bizkit. "Tryna figure out how all this bullshit gon' play out."

"I feel you," said Wesley. "But can't you do it without Cody being in the midst?"

"That's up to him," said Money Mel.

Now all eyes were on Cody as he sat there floating from the effects of the weed he'd smoked. He shrugged under their intense gazes but made no attempt to get up and go with the two men.

"What's it gon' be, son?" asked Corey.

"I'm good," said Cody. "I got thangs to do, and we're wasting time standing around talkin' about it."

Bizkit smirked.

That was all the encouragement Wesley needed to approach Cody and snatch him up onto his feet. In the process, the pistol he had in his lap fell to the floor, and Corey looked absolutely dumbstruck about it. Wesley was quick with the reflex when he saw Cody kneeling down to pick it up. He shoved the boy aside, and Cody stumbled against Lil Earl, almost falling into his lap on the sofa.

Then Corey stepped forward and reached for Cody's arm. "You're coming wit' us," he said.

"Get off me!" Cody pulled away from him, but his father's grip was unbreakable. Corey was a big, solid man; hard time behind the wall hardened him. Man-handling Cody was nothing; it wasn't what he wanted to do, but Cody left him with no other choice.

Although he knew better than to intervene between a father and his son, Dred didn't like what he was seeing and moved in to take action.

"Dred, no!" Lank objected.

"Fuck that shit! The lil' nigga told them what it was from the jump," said Bizkit.

When Dred made it over to them across the room, he grabbed Corey by the arm to stop him. Corey sneered at him, and that was when Cody drew back and punched his father in the face.

"What the!" Corey reached back instinctively, and without hesitation, he hit his son with a vicious right jab to the jaw. The blow stunned Cody, but he didn't bow down to him; he counterattacked and went in on his father with swinging fists.

Pistol in hand, Wesley looked unsure of what to do about the situation. He didn't think Cody had it in him to actually fight back.

"Man, help me break this shit up before they break my shit in here," said Money Mel. Both Dred and Lil Earl moved in to assist him with separating the two, and that was when the unexpected happened.

Cody broke free from his predicament and rushed over to Wesley hard, kneeing him in the nuts and taking the pistol back from him. Then, he whirled around on his father with tears in his eyes, the Ruger pointed directly at his face with his finger on the trigger.

"Chill the fuck out, C." Money Mel saw the look in his eyes and knew what it could lead to.

Cody said, "Leave me alone and get out. I hate you! Go! Go before I shoot you!" His tears were streaming down his gradually swelling face where Corey had hit him. Bizkit's eyes were on the pistol, and it amazed him to see that Cody's hands were steady.

"Don't do this, Cody. We ain't here to hurt you. I'm not," said Wesley, attempting to separate his intentions from Corey's. "Your mama sent us to get you and bring you back home."

"Shut up, Wes! You leave me alone too." Cody swung the Ruger at him next.

"Y'all just go and let the lil nigga do him," said Lank. "You see he ain't tryna be fucked up wit' y'all."

"You ain't my daddy," Cody said to Wesley, then he turned to Corey. "And you ain't my daddy either. I don't got no daddy. So, leave me the hell alone!" he glared.

The crestfallen look Corey presented at the moment was deep to the core.

Cody's words had stung like no other.

It hurt like hell.

Then, without a word, Corey shook his head, turned for the door, and walked back out of the house.

Watching the other man leave quietly, Wesley fought against the agony in his balls and said, "Okay, Cody. How you start is how it ends, baby boy. You've made your choice, and I gotta respect that. But always remember this. The streets ain't loyal, son. You'll see one day."

And then he was gone.

Cody watched Wesley leave without further incident.

"It is what it is," said Lank.

"Y'all ready to bounce?" Lil Earl replied.

With a nonchalant shrug, Cody wiped his face with the back of his hand and said, "Let's ride."

Chapter 11

She was nickin' like a chicken, and Felicia needed to step outside to have a smoke. And that was where she saw Bo Ford, pulling up on the scene in his big F-150 truck. Felicia remained in the shadows, away from the entrance door to which Bo intended to go. She knew why he was there at the hospital — to see Tink Tink, his goddaughter, and to assure Jill that he would do whatever he could to avenge their honor and respect.

Bo Ford was a killer. He'd served in the military years ago before he blew his back out. That was over thirty years ago, and he was still having problems bending at times. But nothing was about to prevent him from getting down to business.

Felicia saw him, and her heart skipped a beat. The Bo Ford she knew didn't back down from anything.

He parked his truck and got out and went inside the hospital and never once glanced her way.

Tossing her cigarette aside, Felicia hurried toward the door and entered, through the lobby and waiting room area, and headed straight for Teddy's room. Shequita was fussing over Teddy, who was up and demanding and so doped up on medication that his words were incoherent.

"Bo just walked in through the front door," said Felicia, and Lisa bolted to her feet immediately.

Not too long ago, Lisa had bumped into Geno Dennis in the hallway. Geno was a good friend of the families on both sides, and he was trying to play peacemaker between the two. He too had been part of Big Boi and Bo's circle before he found God. When they spoke, Geno had informed her that Bo would be making an entrance soon. So, everyone had been expecting his presence, and now that he was here, they wanted him gone.

Also present in the room was Alisha, who Tami was grateful had come. Because if Cody didn't listen to her, at least Alisha would be able to get through to him.

Then, the phone rang as the room buzzed with talk about Bo and what his plans were.

"It's Wes," said Shequita after snatching Tami's phone up off the side table. Teddy was mumbling something as he wallowed in his bed, groaning and carrying on.

Tami took the phone. "What's going on, Wes? Where my son at?" she said.

"You mean our son," came Corey's voice, and Tami sucked in a surprised breath. "He wouldn't come wit' us, Tami. He pulled a gun on us and made us leave the house," he said.

"He did what?" she blurted out. "He pulled a gun on you? Where the fuck is he?!" Tami was mad now, and her forehead began to perspire.

Corey told her how the whole thing went down and then how him and Wesley were falling back to see where the lead would take them.

"Don't let nothing happen to my son."

"He's my son too, Tami," Corey exclaimed evenly. "But me and Wes got it. We got him, Tami," he said.

She sighed deeply and asked him to put Wesley on the phone. Wesley got on and pretty much recapped what Corey said in his own words. Tami was so mad at Cody that she could strangle him.

Wesley said, "They're leaving the house now, baby. I'll keep you posted on everythang."

"You better," she said.

"I love you."

She told him she loved him back and disconnected, her heart burning with emotions on whether she'd lost her son or not.

Alisha's mouth dropped when Tami told them what Cody did. She called Twan and told him where and with who he could find Cody. She wanted him home desperately now. She was actually contemplating going out there to look for him herself.

"It's over," Tami cried miserably.

"What's over, Tee?" Felicia stepped over to place a gentle hand upon her friend's shoulder.

"My baby," said Tami. "I don' lost my baby. I've been a terrible mama. I can't take this no more! I can't!" She ran for the door and snatched it open, but then Tami couldn't leave out of it because someone was blocking her path.

"Going somewhere, Tami?" Bo Ford glared down at her, and Tami could swear she saw blood in his eyes.

~   ~   ~

When Twan received the call from his sister, he was already at the hospital, lurking in the shadows. He already knew Bo Ford was going to eventually show up, had been scoping the scene way before Felicia even came out for a smoke. Twan was with Dale and Rod and their young hooligan, Menace. The plan was already in motion. Dale was already laying in the bed of Bo's truck, strapped with some heavy artillery, waiting for his moment to shine.

When Alisha told Twan who Cody was with, he knew without a shadow of doubt Money Mel was going to see to it that the kid earned his stripes.

He was in capable hands for the time being.

Money Mel was no peon.

He was solid.

But Bo Ford, for the most part, was dangerous, and Twan wanted him nowhere around Alisha or anyone he considered a friend or loved one. So, Twan signaled Rod, and together, they entered the hospital.

Minutes later, Twan was letting himself into the room Teddy was assigned to. And that was where he found Bo, standing toe to toe with Tami, and Felicia was standing right next to her with her fists clenched. It appeared as though the two women were about to pounce on him.

"Do we have a problem?" said Twan, as Rod eased over to Bo's left with his hand close to the Glock tucked at his waistline.

Bo turned to face Twan, and the two men glared at one another. "You damn right we got a problem, homeboy. My partna is dead, and your people got something to do wit' it," he said. "My goddaughter was hurt by your people, and I can't let that slide. Yeah, I said it. I can't let that slide. Somebody gots to pay for the blood that's been spilled," added Bo Ford.

"Is that right?" Twan replied humbly.

"It's only right, Antwan. Yeah. I know all about you and your crew. And your presence supposed to scare me? I've died three times already, and I'm not afraid of death. I've made my peace wit' the Lord already."

"Why do we have to go through this mess?" Alisha replied. "Hasn't enough blood been shed already?"

Bo looked at her and said, "I didn't ask for my partna to be shot and killed. Nor my goddaughter to be hurt in the process. And now Sugar Foot is dead too and Trey barely clinging to life? I didn't ask for any of this foolishness. But it's on me now. I must honor mines," Bo vowed, and Rod snarled in his direction.

"And we will honor our own," said Lisa.

Bo smirked at her. "Do you even feel anythang for Big Boi?" he asked.

"I do, Bo. Really, I do. We went through whatever we went through, but I would have never wished him dead," said Lisa.

"I truly wanna believe that," he said sourly.

Lisa brushed the remark off her shoulders and looked over at Twan in silent resolve.

"I think it's time for you to leave," said Rod.

"I think so too." Bo moved for the door but not without bumping shoulders with Twan on his way out.

"That's really gonna cost him," he muttered. Twan forced himself to keep a level head and not act out for the sake of those occupying the room.

"He was too humble," said Shequita. "I know Bo, and what we just saw meant something to worry about."

"I know," sighed Lisa.

"The calm before the storm," added Felicia.

Twan gave Rod the head signal, and Rod headed for the door next.

"Be careful out there, Twan. I mean it," Alisha said in a shaky voice. Twan nodded and told her that he would take care of it. Then, he was out the door and moving in the opposite direction from which he had come.

He was going to see little Tink Tink and maybe see what Lenny had on his mind too.

An incoming text message alerted him, and Twan retrieved his phone to read it. It was Dale informing him that Bo was on the move. To read that text message confirmed exactly what Twan needed to know — that Bo Ford wasn't on point or else he would have looked in the back of his truck. A man of caution and observation would have detected Dale and probably have sought him harm.

Bo Ford was slipping.

Or so he wanted them to believe. And maybe he was just playing dumb and distancing Dale from them to take him somewhere secluded and murder him. Twan had to think like a killer in order to understand the madness of another killer.

He responded back to Dale promptly.

And then, he phoned Menace to see what his position was. Menace was sharp, he was treacherous, he was worth the confidence Twan had in him.

"I got him in my sights as we speak," Menace answered on the first ring.

"Stay on him, my nigga. Don't blink," he said.

"Say no more, big homie."

Twan had made it to Tink Tink's room door and paused for a moment. Something didn't feel right, and he sensed himself being watched by someone. He scanned his surroundings and guess who he spotted peeping around the corner at him from the hallway?

Detective Raymond Williams. His creepy, so-called discreet observation technique was not as sharp as he thought it was. The nigga ducked off back around the corner like he hadn't just been made.

Twan shook his head and smirked. Then, he turned away from the door and exited the building. Rod was already in the car waiting as he slid into the passenger seat and fired up a fresh blunt.

"Change of plans, brah," he said.

"What?" said Rod. "What you mean change of plans?"

"We let Bo breathe," he replied. "For now."

"But what about Dale?" Rod answered after it registered that Twan actually said what he just heard him say.

Without verbally answering his question, Twan whipped out his phone and sent Dale a quick text to back off and let Bo breathe.

"Too late," said Bo moments later after calling Twan's phone back. "I guess you thought shit was sweet, huh? Now your homeboy got his throat slit."

Twan shut his eyes and labored his breathing.

"I'm coming for you next," Bo growled.

But those were his last words before the sound of automatic rounds hitting his body as Menace's Mac-90 brought him to a bloody death came.

"You still there, big homie?" came Menace's voice moments later after picking up the fallen cell phone.

"What happened?" was all Twan needed to know. But Menace never got the opportunity to explain what happened before he was suddenly ambushed by the authorities.

And that was why Twan called off Bo Ford's demise. Because after seeing the detective, he knew him and his crew were being watched. The town was already hot with the authorities looking for anybody to move wrong, so they could apply some pressure.

Now that pressure had been applied.

"I love you, big homie! But I ain't going out like no chump. These crackas slick, keep tellin' me to put my gun down," said Menace, holding court in the streets. All you heard was gunfire exploding from the other side of the phone.

Then there was none.

And Twan knew the ending.

Young Menace was dead.

Next thing Twan heard was the announcing blurb sound from a police cruiser behind them. Then came the flickering emergency lights illuminating the dark skies around them.

"Shit," Rod muttered under his breath.

All Twan did was shake his head.

"You already know how this gon' play out, brah," he said to his righthand man.

Rod nodded. "Strap tight, my nigga."

"Let's ride," Twan said and pulled out his .45 caliber.

Chapter 12

It was Bizkit, Money Mel, and Cody all in one car while the other three were in the lead. Cody and his team were headed out to find Tysheed. And the second team was going after Bo Ford, not knowing he was already out of commission.

To find Tysheed, he would either be in a splacked (stolen car) or in one of three locations — at this little trap house out in Circle Drive that his big homie, Flip, ran and boomed his dope from. Then, there was his baby mama, Sophia McMillan's crib over in the New Projects, which was where Tysheed was originally from as well. But he'd burned his bridges there with his own people after his thieving crew of hoodlums broke into damn near every home there. Tysheed was the ringleader, but yet he condoned the action, so now he was considered an outsider to his own people. And then there was his other hangout spot over in the Lake Skillet area where he bred his pit bulls.

"Nine times outta ten, Tysheed knows that we know where to find him at and won't be there. He is in the streets right now, lurking just like us," Bizkit replied from the front passenger seat. He and Tysheed shared a level of respect for each other; they were business associates, and Tysheed considered him a young hood legend. Bizkit had earned his stripes at a very young age, and now at twenty-four, his reputation as a gangster was firm.

"Then we improvise," said Money Mel.

"How are we gonna improvise?" asked Cody.

Money Mel said, "We make him come to us instead of wasting time tryna find him. We…" He was cut short by the ringing of Bizkit's phone. "We go after someone he loves dearly."

Bizkit reached for the phone on his lap and answered it speedily when he recognized Lil Earl's number.

"We got your man right now," Lil Earl said.

"My man? Who?" Bizkit passed the blunt back to Cody.

"Who else y'all lookin' for? Meet us at the Pit over in Pepper Hill right now." Lil Earl sounded overly excited about this one.

"I know where the Pit is, brah."

"Then it's understood."

Bizkit hung up with Lil Earl and informed them on what he just found out. How Lil Earl managed to get to Tysheed so fast before them was determined to be revealed.

The Pit was the old neighborhood park on Key Street. It was a place where not much playing went on but a whole lot more street shit, such as crew meetings, a trap spot to hustle, a fuck cut spot on the low, pretty much whatever you wanted it to be. Tonight, it was about to be what it was going to be.

But blood indeed would be shed tonight.

Tysheed might not even get the opportunity to even leave the Pit tonight.

It was a murder mission after all.

Money Mel headed out to the Pit, and Cody wasn't sure if he was actually ready for this.

It didn't take them long to reach the Pit. When they did, the meeting spot was already in order. They got out the car and entered the darkest area of the park, which was back off beyond the basketball court near the rear gate where a shadowy wooded area laid.

Along the street, a lone car drove pass as Wesley and Corey looked in the direction of the darkened park.

"Caught the nigga lackin' at the Kelly Junior store up the street," said Lil Earl. At his feet, Tysheed lay faced down, and the tip of Lil Earl's AK-47 was pressed against the back of his head too.

"He was olo-dolo?" said Bizkit in surprise.

Lil Earl nodded. "I gotta give it to the nigga though. He got heart. When he saw us, he didn't tuck his tail and run," he said. "I respect that shit."

Tysheed was usually with his two closest homies, Zed and Jay Baby, who was also Lank's little cousin. Him and Jay Baby weren't at all close, but the respect was there, and Lank figured one day his cousin would do his part.

Bizkit stepped forward. "Let him up, Dred."

Without question, Dred stepped away from Tysheed as the rest of them circled around him.

"Gimme that gun, Cody," said Bizkit to Cody, and Cody looked up at him with uncertainty. Reluctantly, he handed over his gun, and Bizkit tucked it at his waist behind him. "For future reference, when it's war in the streets, never give up your only protection to nobody. Don't matter who it is. Now you gotta earn that shit back, little nigga."

This is the test, thought Cody. He wasn't sure what Bizkit meant by earning his gun back. Cody looked over at Money Mel, and Money Mel nodded his head in the direction of Tysheed, who was now standing up and looking around at them all cautiously.

"Y'all spread out and make sure that nigga don't run," replied Lil Earl. "Shoot his ass if he do, Dred." The rest of them widened the circle around Tysheed, and Bizkit shoved Cody into the center with him.

"Earn your keep, lil brah," said Money Mel.

When Cody turned toward Tysheed, he didn't even have time to think fast enough. Tysheed rushed him hard and sent three shots to Cody's face, dropping him where he stood amongst them.

"Don't," Bizkit warned Tysheed, who was advancing on Cody to stomp his face into the ground. "Let him get right!"

"No mercy," said Money Mel. "Do what you do."

Bizkit shrugged. "Aight then."

At that, Cody shook away the dizziness in his head and shot up to his feet at once. Tysheed outweighed him by twenty pounds, he was four inches taller, and he was used to throwing hands with the best of them growing up.

This time when Tysheed moved in on Cody, he was ready, and the two collided into each other like two bull rams. Both of them went toe to toe with blows, Cody scared and willing himself to give his all into the battle. He was fighting hard.

"Lil Cody ain't bullshittin'," said Lil Earl.

Money Mel just nodded and watched Cody fight for his life. He was taking some very serious punches from Tysheed. Money Mel was almost ready to stop the fight but knew he had to remain humble.

No mercy, he had said.

No mercy.

Then, Cody was knocked to the ground again, and Tysheed, bloody and dangerous, moved in for the kill. Tysheed rushed in hard and was about to stomp Cody's chest in before Cody grabbed his other leg and yanked him off balance.

This was one of Avery's moves when they used to wrestle in the backyard behind his house. Tysheed hit the ground, and Cody was on him like a tick on a dog.

"Oh, shit!" bellowed Dred when, suddenly, Tysheed, with his longer arm reach, swung a vicious haymaker that landed solidly to Cody's right temple and dazed him.

Tysheed regained dominance and rolled Cody from off of him to replace his position on top.

And that was when the unexpected happened.

The pure savagery and desperation to live.

One swing hitting Cody in his left eye was all it took to bring the beast out of him. The sense of terror and being pummeled to death by Tysheed took Cody from zero to a hundred. Cody lunged forward with all his might that his fear could muster and bit down into Tysheed's neck.

Tysheed screamed.

As fists rained down all over Cody, he sank his teeth deeper into Tysheed's flesh. Tysheed screamed for help as a dark rage took over Cody.

Both Lank and Bizkit looked over at one another. The screams that exploded from Tysheed not only took the fight out of him but it was sure to alert the neighbors in their nearby homes.

"No mercy," Dred muttered with uneasiness.

A burst of desperation swept over Tysheed to try and pull Cody away from him. But Cody was too far gone in his own desperation. Blood gushed into Cody's mouth, making that awakened beast in him feed on the power he now had over Tysheed.

And then Tysheed let out a bloodcurdling cry when he felt a chunk of his flesh break away from his body.

A cold chill ran down Money Mel's spine as he watched Tysheed reach for his throat, writhing in pain and dark fear as his life force left him in spurts of blood spraying in the night air.

~   ~   ~

Just when Twan thought it was about to go down, the cop car swerved around them and charged ahead. He and Rod watched with racing hearts as the cop car blared through traffic and disappeared from sight.

"Damn," sighed Rod. "Thought it was going down just then," he said. "Shit almost got real."

Quietly, Twan reached for his cell phone he had dropped to grab his gun when he thought trouble was coming. His mind was on Dale and Menace and the fate that they had come to tonight.

"I think we need to get off the scene for a minute, my nigga. It's way too hot out here," said Rod.

"We just need to switch cars," Twan suggested.

Rod mulled it over and knew he was right. They had to change their game up. They needed at least three more vehicles at their disposal just in case of an emergency. There was no telling who else knew what they were riding in at that moment. It was too dangerous to be slippin'.

Rod phoned his boy, Yak, and put an order in for two more cars.

"Lemme hit this nigga, Mel, up and see what's good wit' Young C," said Twan. Then, he would check into the Dale and Menace situation. There was a strong uneasiness at the thought of finally telling Dale's grandmother, Connie, that her baby was dead. Then, a deeper depression entered him over how he knew Emma Mae was going to take it when she learned of Menace's death as well.

That was the hardest part — telling the loved ones of the niggas you were committed to thuggin' with that they'd never see them again.

Money Mel sent him to voicemail.

That's that bullshit right there, Twan thought to himself as he hung up the phone.

Then, the phone rang, and Twan gazed down at the screen. He didn't recognize the number but answered it anyway. "Talk to me," he replied.

"Is this Twan?" a woman's voice replied. Twan detected the panic in her voice before he responded.

"Who the fuck is you? What's up?" He wasn't feeling too friendly right now, and Rod looked over at him warily.

"This Meesha from Pole Cat Alley."

"Okay," he waited.

"I got Menace right here wit' me! He's been shot! He told me to call, Twan. I don't know what else to do. I don't know what's going on!" she stressed, and Twan had to calm her down enough to speak with her more humbly.

"Okay. Where are you right now, Meesha?"

She told him.

"Where is he shot?" Twan asked.

"All over," she said.

Damn. "I'm on my way, Meesha! Let him know we coming to him right now!"

"Where to?" Rod demanded. He was ready to whip that muthafucker wherever it was that Menace was being kept in the care of a well-known thot bitch.

When Twan told him, Rod swung the car in the direction of where Menace was fighting for his life.

Then, Twan called Sanda Murphy, one of his side piece's sister, who worked as a registered nurse during the day shift at the local hospital. He told Sand what he needed and promised her the world to make it happen for him.

"This shit is crazy, brah!" Rod said as he pushed the car through traffic, headed toward St. John. "How in the fuck that muthafucker got away like that?!"

"That's Menace," Twan replied.

"Yeah. That little bastard is hard to kill."

Twan shook his head and hoped like hell they made it to him in time.

The last time Menace was shot, he had died twice on his way to the hospital and on the operation table. The nigga had like nine lives like a cat. For some reason, God seemed to spare his life more than others. Him and Menace must have some type of business going on because he wouldn't let that nigga die for nothing. Now Twan was silently praying to that same God to give them a chance to reunite with Menace at least one more time.

Then, he called Money Mel again, and this time, he picked up the phone.

"Tell me something good, Mel. You got Young C wit' you right now?" he asked.

Money Mel said, "I do, but little brah is on some other shit right about now."

"What you mean by that?"

"Brah." Money Mel sighed, troubled by whatever it was that had affected him so. "I know where you stand wit' the lil nigga; that's why I'm not trippin'. But the Cody you once knew ain't the same lil' nigga no more, Twan. Real shit, my nigga."

"What happened?" Twan didn't like the sound of that.

"How 'bout you see for yourself?"

And see he shall.

Chapter 13

Several minutes prior to Money Mel receiving the phone call from Twan the second time, he was about to witness cold-blooded murder by Cody himself. Having watched him fight and bite a chunk of Tysheed's throat out, Money Mel assumed that was the end of Cody's viciousness.

But no, Cody was on autopilot, floating on demon time with a sinister look in his eyes.

By this time, Corey and Wesley had heard the petrified screams from their car parked nearby and came running full speed ahead toward the commotion.

Upon reaching their destination and almost getting shot in the process, Cody had approached Bizkit and demanded his gun back. The whole time, Tysheed was on the ground, wallowing in his own blood and dying slowly.

"You earned it," said Bizkit. When he handed Cody the gun, Cody glared at his face and squeezed the trigger.

Blocka!

One shot to the head was all it took to see what happened when forcing a sleeping lion to awaken and have that same lion end your life in the same breath.

The second Bizkit's brains were blown out the back of his head, Cody spun around on Tysheed and went to stand over his agonizing body next.

"No! Son. Don't do it!" Wesley replied in shock, witnessing what he'd just seen.

Corey didn't say anything because he could already see that Cody was too gone to turn back.

Cody didn't even acknowledge Wesley as he aimed the gun down at Tysheed. From the moonlight overhead shining down from the sky, you could see the fear radiating in Tysheed's eyes as he knew his end had come.

Blocka! Blocka!

Tysheed took his two slugs to the chest and died right where he laid.

"What have y'all done?" muttered Wesley. He looked at Cody and saw the quiet storm raging inside of him. He knew what this moment meant, and it scared him to death to also know that Cody was no longer Cody anymore.

That was when Money Mel drew his second gun and upped them both at Lank and Dred. "Do any one of you niggas got a problem wit' what just happened to Bizkit just now?" he snarled darkly.

At hearing this, Cody swiveled his gaze on Lil Earl, and Lil Earl spoke his peace. He made it loud and clear that Bizkit brought that on himself by forcing Cody's hand to do what he did.

"I feel the same way," said Lank. "It's respect on this side. I fucks wit' the lil' knucklehead."

"Dred?" Money Mel looked at him, unaffected by the assault rifle he had clutched in his hands. He knew Dred was a dangerous nigga, and if given the chance, he would fuck your whole world up.

When Dred didn't answer fast enough to Money Mel's liking, he approached him, but Cody stepped in his path and came face to face with Dred instead.

"Teddy is my brotha — that goes for Mel too — and Bizkit was like family to me, just as much as he was to them and to you. But it was Bizkit who created this monster in me, Dred. It's his fault he's dead. He pushed me, and I pushed back," said Cody.

"You didn't have to kill him though," said Dred. Then, he glared at Money Mel. "Y'all grew up together from the sandbox, Mel. You didn't even try to stop the lil' nigga from…" That was the last thing he said before Cody shot him in the mouth.

"Talks too much." Corey shook his head.

In the distance, the sound of sirens was heard in the night, and that alerted everybody.

"So, we all straight?" asked Lank anxiously as he now felt the need to get as far away from Cody as possible. When it was confirmed that they all were on the same page where Cody's newfound status was concerned, he and Lil Earl hurried up and got missing before somebody else died.

"Let's go!" Corey slapped his son on the back, and to his surprise, Cody nodded, and they hurried away from the scene together.

They all got into the car with Corey at the wheel, and then Money Mel thought fast, knowing that they had to dispose of the car they had come in. When Money Mel jumped back out of the car, Cody followed suit, causing Corey and Wesley to protest to no avail.

Back in the car they came in, Money Mel sped through the back streets of Pepper Hill to distance them from the murder scene.

Then, something happened. Suddenly, Cody began punching the seat under him and burst into tears. He then began sobbing loudly and smacking himself in the side of the head as if trying to knock whatever it was in there that was making him react the way he was at the moment.

Seeing this didn't sit well with Money Mel.

Then, his phone rang.

It was Twan again, but he answered anyway.

The exchange was grim and short as Money Mel shared with Twan what he should know without going into any detail about what transpired.

"How about you see for yourself?" said Money Mel when Twan demanded to know what happened to Cody.

With a deep sigh, Twan said, "I'll hit you back when I'm ready. Got some crucial shit going on on my end right now too."

"I'm here," said Money Mel.

"I know. Y'all stay safe out there."

"You do the same."

"For sho'."

After hanging up with Twan and glancing over at Cody, Money Mel saw that he had ceased his hysterical actions and was quiet now. Cody sat, leaning against the passenger door with his head resting against the window. His eyes were shut, and Money Mel could only imagine what was going through his head at that very moment. What went down tonight would scar Cody forever and affect his future.

In the ashtray was a half smoked blunt of weed they didn't get a chance to finish.

"Here, lil brah." Money Mel offered him the blunt after lighting it up and taking a few pulls from it.

Cody looked up and saw the blunt, then he accepted it and had a healthy lung full of weed smoke.

"Teddy's gonna hate me now," said Cody.

"Naw," said Money Mel. "He won't hate you. He could never hate you, lil' brah. Bizkit made that bed, and now he gotta lay in it. You was outta there, lil' brah. You didn't have time to think. That shit be like that when that demon is released. He brought that shit outta you tonight, and I'm just glad you ain't shoot me too!" said Money Mel further.

Cody didn't reply.

"You snapped into a black rage that was beyond your control, Cody. Now you have to learn to control that demon that's been awakened. It's not easy, but you'll see. You gotta tame that shit, or you gonna self-destruct, and you don't want that happenin'." Money Mel received the blunt back in turn.

Cody said, "You think Lil Earl and Lank really might be a problem?"

"Naw," he said. "Tell you the truth, I think wit' Bizkit dead, them niggas can breathe now."

"What do you mean?"

"I mean, they feared cuz, lil' brah. That nigga was a serious dictator to them fools. Lil Earl, I don' seen him bitch up to cuz too many times. And the nigga, Lank, know what's up. You good. Them niggas won't run they mouths."

"Do you trust them though?"

"I don't trust no one," he exclaimed.

"Not even me?"

Money Mel looked at him for a long moment. "I had always trusted you, Cody, and what happened back there won't change that. You my lil' brah, and I know the reason you sitting there right now is to show your loyalty that you got for Teddy. I got mad love and respect for you, lil' brah. But please, my nigga, please don't let all this shit change who you really are inside." Money Mel reached over and tapped Cody against his solid chest. "I mean in there, Cody."

All Cody could do was nod his head. He understood where he was coming from.

Behind them, somebody hit bright lights, flashing them on and off. It was Corey and Wesley letting them know that they were also there too.

"And that's another thang," said Money Mel.

Cody looked over at him. "What?"

"Your old boy and Wes," he said, "you gotta stop running from the problem and resolve it wit' them."

"I know," Cody sighed. "I already know."

"But not tonight though."

"No?"

"Naw," he assured Cody. "Tonight is all about gettin' to know that beast you just met."

"What beast?"

The look he gave him was stern.

Cody was gone.

His head was not back all the way yet — or if ever.

~   ~   ~

The old, black Impala SS pulled alongside of St. Road and parked behind the sheriff deputy cruiser. Detective Raymond Williams stared through the windshield window for a long moment, looking at the dark, gruesome scene from his vantage point. Then, he got out and made his way over to where two deputies stood off from the dead bodies.

Surprisingly, the crime scene technicians were painstakingly combing over the area while their investigator jotted down in her notepad their findings. Raymond didn't even acknowledge the others as he approached the first body he saw sprawled out on the ground.

"Damn, Sergeant Brentson," muttered the detective as he knelt down next to the dead cop he knew and befriended.

"Got Pete too," said Deputy Ernest Cox, coming over to stand behind the detective. "Can't even recognize him. He took a round to the face."

Raymond glanced up at the deputy and stood. He frowned and turned away from the white man. He bypassed the second dead officer of the law for the big, white Ford truck. A body was hanging down halfway off the side of the truck's rear camper in the back. Raymond stepped up close to the corpse and saw that it was Dale McIntosh from the High Bridge area.

"Another one bites the dust," said Deputy Cox.

"We all will one day," Raymond replied.

"Bo Ford did him in first. We got a witness claiming that he watched Ford park the truck at this stop sign, jump out, and rush to the back of the truck. He struggled with this guy here for a minute, then he killed him and left him where he lay hanging there." Cox was a wide receiver back in his college days, and at forty-two, he looked like he could still suit up. But standing against Raymond's large frame made him look like he could play in the peewee league instead.

"Who's the witness?" he asked.

"A Johnny Gibson," said the deputy. "He lives right there in that house on the corner."

"I know John-John Gibson real good."

After killing Dale, the witness claimed he saw Bo Ford reach over the body into the back of the truck's bed for a cell phone. Then, out of nowhere, came an armed shooter who shot Bo down where he stood.

"Then, Pete and Brent showed up, and the shooter drew down on them too. He killed our guys in a gun battle and hopped into a parked car up the street and zoomed that way," pointed the deputy with an outstretched arm.

"Going into the St. John area?"

The deputy nodded.

"Which means the killer may still be close."

"And he's also injured too."

This startled the detective. "Injured?"

"Apparently, he was shot in the process and still managed to get away. Your guy, Johnny Gibson, can fill you in on what he actually saw. Apparently, he didn't take too kindly having to explain himself to a white man," the deputy replied in a tone of snide and disappointment.

After the detective spoke with John-John Gibson, he knew more than enough to lead from. The injured shooter got away in a dark colored Chevy Caprice Classic.

Back in his car, heading back into town, Detective Raymond Williams told himself that he already knew who the shooter was. He knew the killer was Bernard "Menace" Shaw, one of Twan's loyal homeboys. Which meant that he had one injured severely, one dead, and both Twan and Rod still out there to wreak havoc in what they may deem as retaliation for what had just taken place where two officers were killed.

With two cops dead, the heat in this small town was about to turn into a major furnace.

Raymond wanted no parts of that action if he had anything to do with it because them badges were coming full force, and no one was safe from the wrath that they were about to rain down over the town.

He didn't care for that trouble.

All he wanted was to keep his own ass in check and in place where Tami needed him most.

He couldn't let her down.

Not again.

Chapter 14

Two cars pulled up to a halt outside the house. In the lead car, Tami and Lisa got out, and Alisha exited from her own car behind them. Tami needed a change of scenery. She was going mad being cooped up in the hospital room having to watch how pitiful and agonizing Teddy looked in that bed.

Tami needed to pop some molly and snort a few lines to get her head right.

Felicia and Brandi would call if anything else came up that she should know. In the meantime, Tami had her phone handy and Lisa to keep her company. Shequita thought it was wise that Tami get out and get some fresh air because she was already talking about busting into Tink Tink's room and whipping Jill's ass again plus bringing it to Trey when he got out of surgery. Tami was battling her own conscience as to what she should do or shouldn't do to get back at those who were causing her to lose her damn mind.

"Let's get you in the house," said Lisa as she took the lead, headed for the front door.

"I'll be over in a minute," Alisha said before hurrying over to her own house next door.

But that was before Lisa and Tami noticed that her front door was left hanging off its hinges. Someone had forced themselves through into her house, and that alone had Tami breathing fire.

Suddenly, Lisa gasped in astonishment as Tami materialized with a chrome .380 automatic pistol and charged through the broken front door like a madwoman.

"Where the hell you get that from?!" Lisa wasn't sure whether she should follow her inside. Whoever was responsible for breaking the front door down might still be inside the house, waiting on them to come in.

Lisa glanced over at Alisha's house, seeing that she was already inside her home. Then, she scanned the area of her proximity to see if there was anything threatening lurking about in the night.

"Tami?" She eased toward the door and over the threshold into the foyer. "Homegirl?"

By this time, Tami had switched on all the lights in the house. She was going through every room, looking and searching for anybody who didn't belong there. She had her pistol to guide her and protect her, and Tami was not going to be cowered in her own house.

"Whoever broke into my damn house better be lucky I wasn't here to catch 'em," said Tami.

"It doesn't look like they did anythang though."

"That's because they came here only lookin' for one thang," Tami replied.

Lisa looked up at her in concern. "Cody?"

"My baby." Tami felt her heart begin to pound against her chest again at the thought of somebody breaking into her house to look for Cody and do God knows what to him. The house wasn't ransacked; nothing seemed to have been taken. The mission was to find Cody and Cody only.

"I need a fuckin' drink." Tami didn't head for the kitchen. Instead, her destination was back to her bedroom where she kept her molly stash in the drawer of her nightstand next to her queen-sized bed.

A minute later, Tami was sitting on the edge of her bed, snorting a thick line of crushed up, powdery molly crystals that were laid out on top of a hand mirror. Lisa entered the room just when Tami leaned forward over the mirror to consume the beige substance into the other nostril. Then, she looked up at her homegirl and offered Lisa a shot to get her fix just as she had.

"You know that's my thang too." Lisa took the mirror, dumped out her share from the baggie Tami gave her, made two long lines, and snorted responsibly.

Tami reached into a second bag where an eighth of an ounce of molly broken down in little rocks were and plopped two of them into her mouth.

She gave Lisa only one rock.

When Lisa was messing around with Big Boi, he fed her as much molly as she desired. He had been her constant source and supplier before their relationship went downhill, and she had to let him go.

"Now, it's time for that drink…" Tami replied the instant Alisha appeared in the doorway.

"What happen to the front door?" she asked.

Tami told her.

"Oh, no! I wonder who could it have been." Alisha shook her head wearily.

"Whoever it was is long gone by now, but I know one thang. They better not try that shit again." Tami brandished her pistol and rose up to her feet, and Alisha stared at the little coating of molly residue left at the corner of her left nostril.

"Wipe your nose, Tami."

Tami just shrugged and headed for the door and was enroute to the kitchen when she heard somebody call out to her from the front door.

Tami didn't even bother going to see who it was because she already knew by their voice.

"I'm in the kitchen, Bebop!" she answered. Then, she muttered something slick about her front door being left open for anybody to just walk into her house when that was a major no-no with her beforehand.

Tami was shutting the refrigerator door with her bottle of Hennessy in her hand when little Bebop peeped his little nappy head around the corner at her.

"Come in, you little damn knucklehead! Come tell me what you know about who broke into my damn house." She took a seat at the kitchen counter and preceded to fill a cup with her favorite liquor.

Bebop looked up at Lisa and Alisha's presence and then eased into the kitchen behind them.

This was Byron "Bebop" Jones, a scrawny little knucklehead who was twelve years old and the son of a local crackhead, Peaches Jones, who, ever since Bebop could talk, had never had his mama smile at him. Bebop was a stickler for hood information. He was always watching shit and helping himself to everybody's business in order to earn something for himself. And he was Cody's dear friend, the little brother to him and his crew, and Bebop always managed to find that soft spot in Tami's heart where she couldn't deny him. She had clothed the boy, fed him, whipped his ass, and even bathed him once when he showed up on her front porch looking a mess, like death warmed over and so disgusting that not even Bebop seemed to notice.

Before Lisa could claim the chair across from Tami at the kitchen counter, Bebop hopped up into it and gave Lisa a devilish grin. Then, she thumped him on the top of the head and turned up her nose at the stench of him that was permeating the kitchen around them.

The boy smelled like a grown ass man who hadn't showered in two weeks.

"When you tell me what I need to know, I want you to take your black ass in there and take a bath!" Tami chastised Bebop with a firm tone of voice.

"I'm hungry too," he said.

"You eat something after you bathe," said Alisha. Then, she sparked up the cigarillo pre-rolled blunt of weed that she had brought over with her.

"And I want some weed too," Bebop said.

"You go to hell!" Alisha retorted and moved around the kitchen to find her a glass to drink out of.

"Who broke into my house, Bebop?"

He gazed over at Tami seriously. "It was Flip and Jackpot that did it, Ms. Tee."

"Flip," Lisa said the name sourly.

They all knew who Flip was from over in the Circle Drive territory, a real live wire and the same nigga who was said to have had something to do with his own brother being robbed and killed about a year ago. Word on the streets was Flip had been envious of his brother's street status and had him murdered so that he could take his place.

And Jackpot, there was only one of them in the area, and he was from the Friendship community and had a reputation for breaking into houses. Once when he was fourteen, he was shot in the stomach after he had broken into the wrong house. But that was when he was younger; he was twenty now, and Flip had him hustling drugs for him now. Jackpot had progressed in the game, but yet it turned out that he was still pulling his old stunts again.

And once again, he'd broken into the wrong house. "I got somethin' for them muthafuckas," said Tami.

"Y'all heard about what happen to Bizkit and 'em?" asked Bebop after asking Alisha to pour him something to drink from the fridge.

"Bizkit? What about Bizkit?" asked Lisa.

He told them what he knew.

"What?!" all three women said in unison. "C'mon, Bebop, now you takin' off wit' that bullshit!" said Lisa.

"I'm not lyin'," Bebop confronted.

Without saying a word, Alisha called Twan.

"I heard the gunshots all the way across the neighborhood, then I heard the police coming and rode my bicycle all around till I found 'em at the Pit," he said.

"The Pit?" Tami replied.

He nodded.

"The park up the street?"

Again, he nodded. "I saw 'em wit' my own eyes. I had to sneak through the woods behind the park to really see 'em tho'. It was Bizkit, Dred, and Tysheed."

Now, Tami and Alisha knew why Key Street was blocked off earlier when they were headed back home. There had been patrol cops driving all over the area. Lisa had to take another route to get to the house. Tami too lived on Key Street but farther up the street near the old Steven School Park and Youth Build area, just up the road from the Jackson Heights pool.

When Alisha connected with her brother, she stepped out into the hallway to take her call.

"This shit is unbelievable," whispered Lisa with the shake of her head. "Everybody's dying."

"Bebop?"

He looked up at Tami.

"Go take a bath," she said grimly.

~   ~   ~

"Take me home," said Cody. He and Money Mel had cleared out of Pepper Hill and made their way over into the Sub Division neighborhood where Money Mel's baby mama, Shana, lived with their two-year-old son, Kaedon.

This was also where Wesley, who had followed Money Mel and Cody with Corey to Shana's house, was from. Corey was not trying to let his son out of his sight, especially after witnessing Cody's treacherousness back in the Pit. Corey would never forget that moment as long as he lived.

At the house, Cody watched his father and Wesley pull up and get out behind them.

"I need to talk to you, son," said Corey Williams, a hard man who had a heart of stone, but coming face to face with the monster that was his son scared the shit out of him. Never had Corey been afraid of any man until he saw who his son had become tonight in that neighborhood park.

Remembering the talk him and Money Mel had on their way there, Cody decided to hear his father out and make his decision from there.

Wesley gave them their space while him and Money Mel stepped into the front yard to converse.

"You okay, Cody?"

Cody just looked at him stupidly.

Corey shrugged and said, "That was a dumb question. Of course you ain't okay." He paused for a second and leaned against the side of the car parked at the curb in front of the house. "I'm sorry you had to go through what you did tonight. If I could take it all back, I'd have done it myself to save you, son."

"Save me from what?" Cody questioned.

"The aftermath of what that type of lifestyle would give you from here on out. It's not nice. I know this for a fact, son."

"You talkin' like you killed somebody before."

"Plenty men in my day," said Corey.

"Really, Corey?" Cody gave him a skeptical look. But it was the look that Corey gave him after his son called him by his name that bothered him.

"You got blood on your hands now, son. But that's not really you," said Corey. "You can still take control of your life and make something of yourself. What's it gonna be, son? The choice is yours: the streets or an honest life?" He stared into his son's eyes.

"Just take it one day at a time," Cody told him.

"Good answer. But I'm not here to preach to you, Cody. I just wanna make sure you are still in control. We gon' get through this together."

After their talk, Cody assumed that Wesley had something to say too, but Wesley just nodded at him and hugged Cody. Then, Money Mel took him home after going inside the house to check on his family. The drive back to Pepper Hill was in silence.

Cody was lost in his own mind.

He was troubled.

Fifteen minutes later, Cody was brought home, and they parked behind Alisha's car. Again, Corey and Wesley had followed them back to the house without incident.

"Mama's home," said Cody as he opened the door and got out of the car.

During the same instance, a car turned onto the street up ahead behind Corey and Wesley. They both got out and circled around onto the sidewalk.

And there goes Mama, thought Cody as he watched his mother appear in the doorway of the house. She just stood there, staring out after him, waiting for Cody to finally walk into her arms.

"Get down! Get down!" Money Mel hollered to the top of his lungs just as automatic rounds rang out in the night. "Get down, lil brah."

Startled, Cody turned around to see a car driving past with a gunman hanging out the rear window. Suddenly, he felt two slugs from the unknown shooter's gun strike him in the chest and stomach area. At the same time, Corey was charging toward Cody and tackled him to the ground. Gasping for breath and experiencing intense, excruciating pain from being shot, there was only one thing that stood out to him before everything went totally dark.

It was the sound of his mother screaming over the loud explosions from the exchange of gunfire.

A mother's terrifying cry.

Her ultimate fear.

Chapter 15

Felicia was so emotionally exhausted that she had dozed off sitting in the chair next to Teddy's bed until her cell phone rang, and it brought her up with a start. Glancing around the room and noticing that Shequita was also gone, Felicia got up and went for her phone, which was sitting atop of a table-cart charging from the electrical socket beside the bed.

"Mama?!" Felicia felt her heart quicken at the sound of Avery's voice on the other end of the phone.

"Av!" gasped Felicia.

"Come get me, Mama. I'm in jail. They gave me a five-thousand-dollar bond, but you have to pay ten percent to get me out. That's five hundred dollars, Mama. Please come get me outta this place!"

"But," Felicia had to pause to catch her breath, "what are you doing in jail? I thought they took you and Ava to the Juvenile Detention Center?"

"They did, Mama."

"Then how are you in jail, Av?"

Avery let out an exasperated breath and said, "One of the detention center security guards was tryna rough me up, and so I stabbed him in the eye wit' an ink pen. They took me up to the jail and direct filed me and charged me as an adult, Mama."

"And where is Ava?" she demanded.

He swallowed. "She's still there at the detention center." Felicia wasn't feeling that shit, and she told Avery to sit tight; she was coming to get him.

But first she needed to find Shequita and inform her on what was going on because she would be damned if she left Teddy there alone. That was a no-no.

"Go get Av," came the sound of Teddy's hoarse tone, and she spun on her heels to look at him. Every time Felicia laid eyes on him in the condition that he was in, it made her heart hurt.

"I'm not gonna leave you by yourself, Teddy."

"Where Mama?"

"Don't know where the hell that motha of yours done ran off to," she frowned.

"Go," he said.

"No."

And that was when Teddy eased his hand from beneath the covers to show her the Ruger .32 pistol that his big brother had slipped him on the sly earlier.

"I can take care... myself," Teddy assured her through his agony. Felicia looked at him long and hard, and after coming to terms with where they both stood, she nodded and turned away from him to snatch up her purse and headed for the door at once.

"Love you, Teddy!" she said over her shoulder at him, but Teddy was already gone back under in another deep, medicated sleep. Then, she was out the door and hurrying toward the exit of the hospital.

"Felicia?"

Looking over her shoulder as she neared the exit door, Felicia saw that it was her friend, Margarette Shorter, who she had flown right past in the waiting room area. Margarette was in the company of Jill and Brandi and came rushing over to where Felicia now stood glaring in Jill's direction.

"What're you doing talkin' to that bitch?" Felicia responded the instant they came face to face.

"Tryna learn what's going on around here."

"You could've just come to me and asked!" Felicia shot back at her with a little attitude. "Don't even bother to answer that, Margarette. I gotta go bail my son outta jail right now," she said hastily.

"Avery?"

Felicia nodded.

And that was when it finally registered that she hadn't come to the hospital in her own car. She had accompanied Tami and Wesley there, riding in their car. Her old Nissan was still parked in her driveway at home.

"I need to get to the Leon County Jailhouse," Felicia swallowed her pride and said.

"That's where he's at, Felicia?"

She nodded.

"Then let's go get him!" said Margarette.

Felicia let her lead the way and followed her out of the hospital with her heart bleeding for her son and her precious daughter.

~   ~   ~

Twan hated having to ignore his sister's phone call, but if she was calling from her own phone, nine times out of ten, she was good. She was alive and probably being the worry-sister that she was, just wanting to get an update on what he had going on.

When Alisha called, Twan had just made it to Meesha's house out in St. John. He had gotten there ten minutes after Sand had arrived with her faithful assistant and all the works that were needed to make a successful mission.

Menace had suffered two gunshot wounds to the shoulder and a through and through wound in the stomach. By the time Twan and Rod got there, Sand already had an IV tube attached to his arm, a breathing oxygen mask over his face, her assistant, Kim, sanitizing the medical utensils that were needed to perform surgery, and Menace dozing off from the heavy sedation that was administered to him.

After fifteen years in the medical field as an LPN and a surgeon's assistant, Sand knew exactly what she was doing to try and save Menace's life.

Behind the scenes, it was Sand who a lot of street dudes and others alike had gone to when it was too critical to deal with the paperwork at a hospital. There was some she couldn't save but a whole lot more that were very gracious toward her hasty performance and dedication to emerge victoriously. It was Twan who had convinced her to open up her own lowkey practice and take care of those who wanted to keep shit on the hush.

Twan funded her mission initially, and now Sand's hard work and dedication had earned her more money than she would have ever imagined having.

The streets made sure of that, and Sand didn't hesitate to get her job done.

Meanwhile, Meesha was beyond panic-stricken; she didn't know what to do. Twan found her in her kitchen, smoking a molly-laced blunt of weed and nursing a can of Pepsi and mumbling softly to herself. When he entered the room, she flinched as if afraid Twan would harm her, but he reassured her that he was grateful for her help.

"Is he gonna live?" asked Meesha.

"I believe so, yeah. My girl, Sand, and her assistant are good at what they do," said Twan.

Meesha took another healthy drag from her blunt. "He tell you who shot him?"

"That's what I wanna talk to you about."

"I don't know nothin'!" She panicked, and Twan reached across the table for her hand. "I got two children, Twan. I don't wanna be…"

"Calm down, Meesha. You don't got nothin' to worry about. You are safe. Your kids too. But you must promise me that you won't speak on what happen t'night. I need your word on that, Meesha."

She looked so scared. To Twan, she looked like she was about to jump up and flee from him. There she was, a well-known thot bitch who flirted with danger fuckin' with a fleet of different niggas on an everyday basis without a care in the world, niggas so dangerous that Meesha knew she was taking a chance on getting caught in the crossfire when some deadly shit popped off.

Meesha was a con artist as well, and Twan assumed her actions were just a role she was playing to gain his affection and his sympathy.

Twan pulled his hand back when he felt Meesha caressing it a little too much.

"I won't tell nobody," she said evenly. Twan wasn't sure where her thoughts were when she made that statement. "I just don't want no trouble comin' to me and my children behind that shit."

"I'll make sure that it won't."

"You promise?"

Without words, Twan reached into his coat pocket and pulled out a thick roll of cash money. He then rolled it across the table to her, and Meesha damn near threw her arm out the socket reaching for the money. "Thank you."

"That's some real shit right there, Twan."

He nodded and rose to go check on Menace and make sure Rod had his end covered.

"Um, Twan?"

He was halfway out the kitchen when he stopped and gazed back at her. "Yeah?"

Meesha licked her big, juicy lips seductively, and Twan saw that twinkle in her eyes. "Whenever you need a real headhunter to getcha right, you know you can always call me," she said smoothly.

"I'll keep that in mind." Twan smirked and turned away from her back for the den area of the house he couldn't wait to be out of.

Sand, white lab coat on with surgical gloves and surgical face mask, was still performing Menace's surgery, extracting the slug from his shoulder while Kim held the strobe light over them for her to see. It was so quiet in the room that Twan was afraid to say anything. Plus, he didn't want to distract her from her job and went to go look for Rod.

Rod was standing out front on the phone, talking to his brother, Meatball, another go-getter and bonafide killer who left home years ago to go build his own life down in Tampa. Meatball was the truth, smart as hell but a little off the charts as well.

When Rod looked up and saw Twan, he gave him the patient finger — give him a minute and he would be right with him.

But Twan was already reaching for his phone when he felt it vibrate in his front right pocket.

It was his sister.

"My fault for not hittin' you back earlier, sis. I was in the middle of some crucial shit," he said.

From the other end of the phone, all Twan heard was somebody sobbing miserably in his ear.

"Lisha?" he replied.

More crying was his answer.

Rod ended his call and turned to his righthand man and noticed the disturbing look on his face. "What is it, my nigga?" he spoke up.

"Alisha. What's wrong, sis? Talk to me before I act the fuck up! Why you cryin'?" Twan was growing angry and worried for his beloved sister.

"Antwan? This you, baby?" Another voice came over the phone, and Twan felt a cold chill travel through him at the premonition of something very troubling.

"It's me," he swallowed.

100

"Oh, Lord, Antwan. I'm wit' your sista. She's been shot, baby. She was callin' you… I think to tell you that she loves you. I'm so sorry, baby."

Something shattered inside of Twan at hearing those words that Lisa had spoken.

"So, what're you saying?" Twan said through gritted teeth.

"She's… gone, Antwan. Alisha is dead."

The instant those words left her mouth came the sound of Twan's phone breaking into pieces as his hand unconsciously clenched into a maddening fist. And then something in him snapped. Twan stumbled back as though being struck by a punching blow. Then, he fell to his knees and roared like the lion which he was.

"Oh, shit," was all Rod could say.

He knew.

Alisha was gone.

And so was the sanity of Antwan Young as the streets now better beware of the pure hell he was about to bring down upon them.

Chapter 16

When Cody finally came to, he opened his eyes at the very same time he felt the splash of his mother's tears falling upon his face. He had been lying in her arms as she wailed like a brokenhearted child. Then, the pain erupted through him that caused Cody to cry out in absolute agony.

When Tami heard this, she froze, gazed down upon her son, and screamed in surprise and relief that Cody was not dead.

"I'm here, baby. Mama's right here wit' you, baby. Don't be scared. I gotcha, baby." Tami resumed rocking her son back-and-forth in her arms. It reminded you of that scene on *Set It Off* when TeeTee was dying in the backseat of the car in her best friend's arms after being shot during a bank robbery. That was how Tami looked as Cody lay writhing in pain and agony in her arms right there in their front yard.

Through his pain, Cody looked around him and saw all the horror that surrounded him.

"No! No! No!" he bellowed at the sight of his dead father lying in the grass two feet from where he also laid. During the attempt at saving his son's life by using his own body as a shield, Corey had taken a slug through his back that killed him on the spot.

That beast in Cody roared.

Cody breathed harshly, his chest rising and falling in an effort to hold back his deep, dark rage. Then, his gaze swiveled over to Wesley and saw him laid out on the front lawn, dead too. His brain was filled with a red haze, a dark edged rage and fierce hunger for revenge for those he lost.

"Baby?!" Tami reached out for him as Cody gritted his teeth and bolted up to his feet so suddenly that his elbow struck her in the forehead.

From the sidewalk came Money Mel, holding his side and clutching his burner. Cody stared down at himself and spotted two holes in his shirt where the velcro vest had stopped the slugs. The bulletproof vest was indeed a lifesaver.

"Cody," came the familiar sound of Bebop's voice as he stood in the doorway of the house.

When Cody saw Bebop standing, he rushed over toward him, stopped midway, turned back for his scared-looking mother, took her by the hand, and pulled her along with him.

"I thought you was dead, baby," she said as he dragged her toward the front door of the house. "You need to see a doctor, Cody. You're hurt."

"I'm good!" Cody assured her.

Bebop remained standing in the doorway, half naked, and then Cody shoved him backwards into the house. He pulled Tami along and glanced out at Money Mel, who was moving unhurriedly toward him.

And that was when they heard Lisa sobbing somewhere in the house, and Tami rushed in to go see what was wrong.

"What're you doing, Bebop?" Cody glared down at the frightened boy.

"Helpin' yo' mama and 'em," he answered. Then, Bebop shuddered and said, "Alisha got shot too."

"What?!"

That was when Cody heard his mother scream.

"Mama." Cody instantly spun on his feet to run to his mother, and then his knees buckled under him. He fell to one knee, gasping and groaning in agony, clutching his chest area where one of the bullets struck him. "Ma," he gasped again, and Bebop touched his shoulder.

"Alisha got killed," said Bebop. "That's why yo' mama cryin', Cody. She dead," he added.

Money Mel came through the front door and leaned down to check on Cody. He asked what was wrong, and Cody told him fitfully.

"You gon' have to fight that shit for now, Cody. I know how bad it hurts. I got hit too. Get the fuck up! We gotta get them somewhere else safer," said Money Mel.

That moment of grinding out the pain came for Cody as he moved through the house and found Alisha in the kitchen. Somehow, she got hit by a stray bullet that traveled through the thin walls of the house. The bullet struck her in the head, and she died.

Later on, Lisa would state how after being shot in the head, Alisha managed to pull out her phone and call her beloved brother.

Both Tami and Lisa were in severe panic mode. When Cody went to his mother, it was her who told him that he needed to leave before the police came.

"I'll take care of the house," Tami told her son.

"But you're not safe here, Mama."

"Yes, I am," said Tami. "Now take your ass out there and get the muthafuckas who did this. You the man now, baby. Go take care of your business!" She hugged him, and Cody damn near screamed from the pain in his chest and his stomach. "I'ma be aight, baby. Now go!"

The shocked expression on Cody's face said it all. The last thing he would have ever imagine his mother saying was just said. She literally told him to go out there and earn his stripes.

To go kill somebody.

Little did she know, he'd already killed three people tonight and his stripes already earned in the faces of those whose reputation was already solidified.

"Can I go wit' you?" Bebop asked. Cody was just about to say something before he sensed another presence behind him.

Then came the alarming sound of police sirens coming near to see what all the fuss was about.

Cody turned around and standing before him was none other than Po'Boy. Earlier at Money Mel's crib before Wesley and Corey showed up, Po'Boy had received an emergency phone call and had to leave. Now there he was again, back like he never left.

This was Money Mel's road dawg; him and Po'Boy were closer than him and Bizkit were. It was Po'Boy who Money Mel had called back at Shana's crib to come thug it out with them.

"So, what's the game plan…" Po'Boy was stopped short of whatever he was saying when he gazed across the room and saw Alisha's dead body on the floor.

Po'Boy looked sick all of a sudden.

"Oh, shit, y'all. That nigga, Twan, finna go slap-crazy 'bout that shit," he said slowly.

Cody broke away from them and pulled Bebop with him. Bebop felt like he was about to be retribution for being there tonight. This was a whole different type of Cody he was used to dealing with.

"You wanna do somethin' to help me, Bebop?" Cody asked the boy who stood before him in just a pair of dirty Spider-Man drawers.

"Yeah. You my big brotha. I can help."

Cody said, "Stay here and watch over my mama for me. Don't let nothin' happen to her, Bebop. I'm counting on you to do that for me, little brotha."

"Can I have a gun then?" said Bebop.

"No!"

"But you got one," Bebop whined.

"I said no, Bebop!"

The boy let out a frustrated sigh and nodded his head, then he said, "Don't get killed too, Cody." Bebop's bottom lip trembled as if he was about to cry.

"One time!" Money Mel called out, and suddenly, everybody became frantic that the police had come.

"Back door. Hurry up! Go," shouted Tami, and the fellas bounced for the back exit at once. Two cop cars were pulling up out front of the house where two dead bodies lay sprawled out in the front yard.

After seeing her son, Tami rushed back to her bedroom where her drug stash was. She was not about to risk the cops discovering her stash when they started trampling all over her house.

Tami stuffed the stash down into the front of her panties and put her game face on.

It was one helluva night.

A bloody one indeed.

~   ~   ~

How stupid it was for Geno to tell Shequita that her son was also being said to have had something to do with Big Boi's murder. That he was spotted leaving the house along with others after Big Boi was killed.

Geno claimed he got this information from Lenny Davis, and Lenny heard it first from his daughter, Tink Tink. Now, Shequita felt crossed and figured she needed to do something about that.

But of course, Geno Dennis, the peacemaker between the two families, preached to Shequita how critical it would be for her to go off the deep end. That she needed to remain humble and let him settle the matter. Over the course of the past twenty years or so, Geno had been a great help and friend between the two families. He had always been there when they needed a voice of reason and someone who stood firm on what was right. But after looking in Shequita's eyes and seeing the fire ablaze in them, Geno very much doubted he could persuade her to remain steadfast and let him do his general part.

Shequita was beyond reasoning when her son was in danger and her very own existence was jeopardized.

She was a mother scorned.

Mama was fed up.

So, when Geno made his third trip down the hall to counsel with Lenny and Jill Davis about the situation, Shequita had slipped out of the room next. She had learned from Brandi that Trey was out of surgery and had been put into the severe ICU ward while under law enforcement watch. Which meant his situation warranted for him to be guarded by a government official until further notice. Apparently, he wasn't only just a victim but a criminal too, one that was found under grave conditions but still considered a threat to society.

Trey had taken several bullets tonight and was laid up in the ICU ward in critical condition, barely hanging on to life. And Shequita didn't care none whatsoever; she needed to make sure he never lived to seek vengeance.

Trey had to die.

But when Shequita spotted two cops hanging outside his room door, she returned back to Teddy's room. There she found Felicia gone, but she still had to figure out a way to get to Trey.

Shequita had never killed anyone a day in her life. She came closer to killing Tim, who was her children's father, and not even then could she muster up the strength to do it.

Timothy Anderson had been a cruel man, but now cancer was eating his ass up inside.

How cruel was that?

Plus, Tim had a mental problem. He was schizophrenic and suffered from PTSD. But he hadn't always been a bad man. Once upon a time, Shequita had worshipped the ground he walked on. He had been her high school sweetheart, then he graduated and enlisted to the Army, leaving her home to care for their unborn child, Money Mel. Then, years later, he was discharged from service due to mental issues and came home to her and his son. Then, Shequita got pregnant again, and that was when she really started noticing the change in Tim. First, it started off with verbal abuse, then once that began to not affect her anymore, he started to put his hands on her. He had even sent her to that very hospital quite a few times for her injuries. His cruel performances had stretched longer than it should have, only because Shequita loved him so and convinced herself that she could change him.

That was before Teddy got fed up with him hurting her and took matters in his own hands. Teddy was just eight years old when he stabbed Tim in the stomach with that butcher knife. Tim would have died that night if Shequita hadn't rushed him to the hospital. And that very same night, both of her children cornered her in the hospital room and demanded that she leave their father. During this time, Money Mel had found Tim's old .357 Magnum and held it against his father's head, threatening to pull the trigger if she didn't call it quits with Tim.

That night, Shequita made the ultimate sacrifice.

Tim was left alone.

Sometime later, after futile attempts to come back home, Tim relocated to Jacksonville, Florida and never returned to Quincy for any reason. He had made himself another family, with a wife and daughter, and Shequita was grudgingly happy for him.

But then, when the door opened and Timothy Anderson was pushed in by that very same woman who was his wife, Marolyn, Shequita damn near went into cardiac arrest at the sight of the man.

Her real-life monster was here in the flesh. In a wheelchair.

And still, Tim looked every bit of the cruel man that she remembered him as.

But this version of him was more hideous.

Chapter 17

Tim Anderson had been one of the largest human beings Shequita had ever known growing up. Now he looked like someone had deflated him to barely a third of his former size. Tim's skin was very much darker now; he used to be of a pecan tan complexion. Back when they were in high school, folks in Quincy would come to cheer him and the James A. Shanks Tigers football team on during every game. Tim had been the powerful running back that took the Tigers to two championships. Even when he enlisted to the Army, he had left big and powerful and returned even more the large and ruthless man that he turned out to be.

Tonight, Tim entered the room in a pair of slacks, T-shirt, and an old, tattered leather coat that Shequita remembered him owning. His short hair was sprinkled with gray. His face was gaunt, his sunken chest drawing in and out in slow, elongated motions. Tim was perspired with sweat on his face and not much life in his deep brown eyes.

Shequita felt her heart thump with emotion as Marolyn wheeled her husband in closer. There was an oxygen tank tucked in the back compartment behind his chair, its attached lines running up to his nostrils. Tim Anderson seemed to suck desperately on the air it gave.

Wheezing, Tim said, "I made Marolyn bring me as soon as I heard what happened."

"Who told you?" asked Shequita. She knew her oldest son had been to visit him earlier today, but that was before all the bullshit jumped off.

"Gotta call from an old friend of a friend who told me everythang."

Shequita thought for a moment. "Randy?"

He nodded.

"Well. You heard about what happened to Randy too, right? It's become a never-ending cycle of killings around here, and nobody can't seem to do anythang about it."

"I can," said Tim.

"Yeah, right," Shequita frowned. "What the hell can you possible do right now, Tim?"

"Make amends wit' my boys — and you," he said.

"It's way too late for that bullshit, Tim. None of that would change the fact that my son is lying in that hospital bed right now in pain."

"He's my son too." For some reason, hearing him say that made her cringe inside. Then, Tim shifted his withered body a bit, so he could sit up straighter in his wheelchair. His features were somber. "I only have so much time left to live, and I want to go doing something meaningful, Quita. Me and Marolyn already fought over it on the ride here. There's nothin that's gonna convince me not to at least show my love for my sons — and my undying love to you — by doing what I came here to do," he said.

"To make your sorry amends, right?"

"More than that, Quita."

The look on Marolyn's face was grim. She was a very pretty woman with a no nonsense air about herself, but there was a drain of hope in her eyes that obviously came from the reality she was now faced with.

Shequita sensed something sinister interpreted from Tim's words of expression. She read it in his eyes, and the mischief she saw in them gave her pause.

110

"I know all about young Trey and what he has been up to in regard to my sons' wellbeing," said Tim. "And I know it bothers you having him so close but can't touch him."

"What're you talking about, Tim?!"

"You know exactly what I'm talking about, Quita. It's time I do what I have to do to protect my own."

"Marolyn? Really?" Shequita stared up at the other woman standing before her. "Are you hearing him right now? Do you even care?"

"I'm just doing my part as a devoted wife."

"And you support that?"

"He's my husband," she said simply. "And I'll never step between a man and his mission to protect his children. It's a hard pill to swallow, I know. But whatever makes my man proud and happy, I will stand by it."

And how could Shequita argue with that when she once felt the same way about that very same man?

"Am I wrong?" said Tim.

Shequita looked at him intensely.

He is not wrong, thought Shequita. If he wanted to go out with a bang by killing Trey, then by all means she wasn't going to stop him.

"So, what's your plan, Timothy?" she asked.

A crooked grin spread over his clumsy face. "I thought you'd never ask."

~   ~   ~

Po'Boy, being the cautious nigga he was, had parked his car along a side street nearby and footed it the rest of the way to reach Cody's crib. He had seen the cop cars lurking through the neighborhood, searching for anybody and anything to catch slipping.

Po'Boy led the way through some neighbors' backyards, over a fence, and through a known path that brought them to a parked car on Old Stevenson Road. It was a stolen, four-

111

door Mazda that he'd spliced from the car dealership over by the Winn-Dixie downtown.

They got in the car, and just as Po'Boy pulled out, they saw Twan shooting past them along the street. If the Mazda's headlights wouldn't have been on bright, Money Mel never would have spotted him.

"He's going to my house," Cody said.

"We should go try and stop him."

"Think that's a good idea?" Po'Boy looked over at Money Mel and asked.

It would be a dangerous task to return back to the house now after what all that had happened. Then, Money Mel called Tami's phone to forewarn her that Twan was headed their way now.

"I got him," she told Money Mel. "I know what to do wit' Antwan."

"He's not thinking straight, Ms. Tee."

"Me neither," she said and disconnected, causing Money Mel to hope like hell Twan didn't do something stupid to get himself jammed.

"So, what now?" Po'Boy said impatiently.

"I know I hit one of them niggas who was shooting at us," said Money Mel. "And if I'm not mistaken, I think it was that clown ass nigga, Zed. He was the one hangin' out the window shootin'."

"Which means Jay Baby or somebody else was the driver. Which means regardless of who it was, Jay Baby gonna get bust too, and we might have to deal wit' my nigga, Lank, about his people," Po'Boy said as he swerved the car onto MLK Boulevard, heading toward the Lake Skillet area.

"Call Lank and see what he can do," suggested Cody and winced from his chest agony.

"What the fuck can Lank do? Three muthafuckas died because of them t'night. Either Lank gotta get wit' the program or get smoked t'night too. I don't wanna do it, but it is what it is. My loyalty is wit' you, Mel," said Po'Boy.

A second later, Money Mel's phone rang, and he was surprised to see Twan's number. He did not even hesitate answering. "What's up, Twan?"

"Where you at?" came his deep, menacing baritone.

"Wherever you need me to be, my nigga."

"Tami said you might know who murdered my sista."

"I do."

"Then you call the spot."

Money Mel thought about it for a second, glanced through the windshield, then said, "I'll be over at the Complex across from the New Projects."

"Say no more."

"And Twan?"

"Yeah."

"I'm sorry, big brah," said Money Mel.

The line disconnected.

With a shake of his head, Po'Boy spoke up and commented on what he felt about the situation. He was wary about Twan's intentions and warned them that they should exercise their cautiousness.

During this moment, Cody was in the backseat, holding his chest and trying not to breathe too hard. He wanted to take the vest off, so he could breathe more easily. And that was exactly what he did. Cody struggled with the effort of relieving himself of the vest. When he finally had it off, he allowed himself a moment of great relief.

"I know, right?" said Money Mel when he glanced back at Cody and noticed his expression.

Cody didn't reply.

They made it to the Complex, which was the baseball and softball park and playground for the community events. It was an area where the car shows were hosted, parties, and more where one could go and make things happen when needed.

Like now, as Po'Boy turned into the entrance of the Complex, there were three other individuals already hanging out there, smokin' and chillin'.

"That's Shane and Monsta and PJ right there," said Po'Boy, relieved to see that the trio was his very own Lake Skillet crew members. These were his homeboys, and with Shane being his cousin, Po'Boy didn't need to worry too much about the situation.

The Mazda pulled right up to the three niggas hanging out by the situation building structure.

"What you fools doing out here?" Po'Boy said when he got out the car.

"Oh, shit! What's up, cuz?!" Shane replied. He passed the blunt over to PJ and hurried over to meet Po'Boy.

While Po'Boy conferred with his cousin, Money Mel and Cody remained close to the car. Cody was now shirtless as he stepped around the car toward Money Mel, who was checking the magazine of his Glock.

"War wounds," said Money Mel when he spotted the two intensively sensitive dark spots along Cody's chest and stomach. "Hurt like a muthafucka, huh?"

"Hell yeah," said Cody.

"I caught one in the side too. I think it cracked one of my ribs."

"Then I know that shit hurts too."

"I'm alive."

"Yeah," Cody shrugged. "I'm still alive." He glanced in the direction of the others and saw that Shane was looking directly at him from ten feet away. He was about to question Money Mel about the others when the roar of a car's engine stole his attention.

"There he goes," muttered Money Mel. They watched as the big car swung into the entrance of the Complex and charged right for them. The car slammed on brakes beside the Mazda, and Twan jumped out from behind the wheel like a lion from its cage.

"Young C," Twan acknowledged him first and walked up to Cody and examined his visible gunshot wounds and frowned deeply. "You good?"

"No."

"Me either. But we all we got now, and I just want you to know that Alisha loved you like a little brotha. She's the one that called me up to come look for you out there in them trenches. Now my sista is gone, and I'm not taking that loss quietly," said Twan.

"I don't expect you to, Twan."

Money Mel said, "We might have an issue wit' one of our own." He went about sharing with Twan what took place back in the hood and who their targets were. "I don't mind puttin' his lights out."

"You spoke wit' Lank already?" asked Rod. He was cool with Lank — so was Twan and them all — but blood connection was involved now, and there was no tellin' how Lank wanted to play it.

"Maybe I should've killed him too when I had the chance," said Cody.

"Too?" Twan looked over at Cody in astonishment. "What you mean you shoulda killed him too?"

That was Po'Boy's cue to say, "Oh. You ain't heard the news about Bizkit and 'em?"

"I heard. Why?"

Then Po'Boy gestured toward Cody without verbally saying what Twan refused to believe.

"That's your work?" Twan replied.

"I had no choice, Twan." Cody told him about Bizkit and his hand being forced to battle Tysheed and then the extermination of the others. Twan couldn't believe what he was hearing and gazed back down at the two bruises along his body. Then, there was no doubt in his mind what he heard was true. Because once he looked in Cody's eyes, he saw that familiar story of a killer and his mission.

"Damn, Young C." Twan shook his head. "Then you already know what it's gon' be from here on out?"

"I'm ready," Cody replied.

Twan gripped his shoulder and said, "Aight. We gon' take it to them niggas. But outta respect for Lank, my nigga, I wanna see how he gonna play this shit out."

"So, we call him up?" said Cody.

Suddenly, Monsta came over to stand among them with his phone in his hand. "You might don't have to do that because I just got word on Zed's whereabouts. He's over in Lake Skillet right now. They just pulled up to Flip's crib not too long ago," he said.

"Tysheed's hangout spot," Money Mel pointed out.

Po'Boy nodded. "Then there you have it. Let's go punish them niggas," he expressed.

You didn't have to tell Twan twice because he took off running through the Complex for the Lake Skillet community which was just across the street. There was no mistaking what his intentions were when he reached Flip's house around the way.

Chapter 18

Tami was on her back porch, smoking a Newport, when the back door opened, and Raymond Williams stepped out. She gazed back at him and let out a troubled breath. Another pull from her cigarette and Tami exhaled a cloud of smoke into the air.

Detective Williams turned toward Tami and joined her on the porch step but not without removing his gold badge from his hip and tossing it out into the shadows of the backyard.

"Don't know what you did all that shit for, Ray." Tami didn't even look his way as she spoke. "When I asked you to do that years ago, you made me seem as if I was talkin' to a brick wall," she continued with conviction.

"I know you're hurtin', Tami," he said.

"I lost two men I loved t'night and a very, very good friend of mines. And now I've gone and told our son to go avenge the deaths of the lives that was taken before our eyes t'night."

Ray shivered at her words.

"A father he thought was his and never even knew the truth. A man he'd grown to hate and dislike when it should have been you, Ray. Your son has been in desperate need of your love and strength and never once did you even attempt to try."

"So, you're blaming me for what's happened?"

"Yes," she replied. "I am."

"But yet you knew my situation then, and you damn sure know my situation now." Ray said this with a hint of irritation and turned his hard gaze on her and said, "We had an arrangement, Tami."

"Yeah. Right. First it was your marriage to Latrice Goodman that our affair would have destroyed your chance wit' kissin' up to her chief of police daddy, who did eventually help you climb up in rank. And now that you are who you are, it's not safe for you to be the father Cody needs in his life. You say it's too dangerous and that your 'enemies' would try to use our son to get to you." Tami then looked over at him with a hard expression. "I still can't believe I let you talk me into agreeing to that bullshit all these years," she snapped.

"I still did my part though, Tami."

"It wasn't enough."

"Okay. So, what do you want me to do, Tami? Fuck it! You want me to throw everything away for someone who'll end up hatin' me just as well? Is that what you want, Tami? Goddamn." Ray shot up to his feet and descended the three steps down onto the ground. Then, he began to pace the earth back-and-forth like a worried hyena.

"Cody lost two fathers t'night," she said. "And now it's time for his real father to step up."

"So, it's fuck my life?"

"It's fuck his life then, Ray? I swear to God if I had a gun, I'll…" Tami cut her words off when the back door suddenly opened, and a plain clothes police investigator peeked her head out and beckoned for Detective Raymond Williams. He glanced at Tami, and Tami gave him that stern look that he knew all so very well.

"What is it, Patricia?" he acknowledged the older, Black woman investigator, avoiding having to look at Tami and seeing the way she looked at him.

"You're not responding to your communication, Sarge."

He examined his person carefully. "I guess I left it in my car. What is the problem?"

"There's been another death reported, sir."

"And the extent of this incident?"

Tami rolled her eyes.

"Over at the local hospital. The victim's Treyvon Conyers, a recent inpatient victim of another shootin' tonight. Well, he was just murdered in his room in the ICU ward while under protective custody."

"What?!" Ray gasped in shock.

"Oh, Lord," whispered Tami. She stressed over whether it was Shequita or Felicia or anyone else she cared about who had been the one to kill Trey.

That was like the tenth killing tonight, and Tami feared it was so much more to come.

This caused Ray to go in a frenzy and leave Tami there, sitting alone in her misery. She then flicked her cigarette away and made her way down the porch steps. Then, she searched the area along the backyard for a minute until she found what she was looking for.

"And here's the reason why." Tami stared down at the gleaming gold badge in her hand. What she now possessed was evidence of why she couldn't share a proper life with the man she really wanted.

Cody's real father.

If only he had committed his love and life to her then maybe she wouldn't be hurting right now. And just maybe Cody would be really happy for a change.

~   ~   ~

It was 11:14 p.m. when Felicia returned back to the hospital with her son in tow. Avery looked tired and anxious, and Felicia, gripping his hand in her own, refused to let him go for any reason. Margarette was doing her best to keep up with Felicia's long legs and her rush to return back to her loved ones. Avery was dressed in the same clothes he had been in when he and his twin pounced on Tink Tink and her best friend, Breanna. There were specks of blood on his shirt and pants from the incident.

When they arrived inside the room, Felicia was instantly struck with curiosity as to who the stranger was occupying the room with them.

Avery pulled away from his mother and rushed over to Teddy's bedside at once.

"This is Marolyn," said Shequita with a look of bewilderment etched on her serious face. "She's Tim's wife. They're here on behalf of Teddy's situation."

"So, where the hell is Tim?" demanded Felicia.

Before anyone could answer, the whole building suddenly awakened with the startling blare of the fire alarm going off throughout the hospital.

"What the…" Felicia froze.

"Don't panic," Shequita replied humbly.

It was the way in which she said it that made Felicia regard her friend suspiciously.

"It's all just part of the plan," said Shequita.

"Plan? What fuckin' plan?" snapped Felicia, moving over to stand closer to her son. The door opened, and Brandi slipped inside the room. "What's going on out there? Is the building on fire or something?"

"Or something," Brandi repeated.

Over the loud commotion of the fire alarm and people running about the hallways of the hospital in a frenzy, Teddy had pulled Avery close to tell him something in his ear. It was as if they were conspiring on something, and with the way Teddy looked at the moment, that something was obviously not anything good.

Meanwhile, Shequita explained to her friend what Tim had left the room on his own to go do.

Felicia looked dumbfounded about what she had been told and knew the truth laid in what was happening right now.

"And you're down wit' all of this?" She turned to Marolyn.

"It's his dying duty to fight one last war." Marolyn said this as though she'd practiced it.

One last war. A final battle. One more chance to earn his rightful glory.

Because at that very moment in time, Timothy Anderson was using what strength he had left to execute his plan of attack. For those who knew and believed, he would not be returning back to the room. He had already made his claim to die, and by all means, he was sacrificing his life for his own.

The wait was crucial.

Then came the two unmistakable gunshots that indicated the end of the battle. The end of Tim Anderson. Another dead soldier who fought hard for his country and those he loved.

A river of tears spilled from Marolyn's eyes, and it was all Shequita could take before she pulled the other woman into her arms.

"It's over," whispered Shequita.

Waiting for that ending was like waiting to watch a loved one take the lethal injection for a crime he didn't do. It was devastating waiting and knowing it was going to hurt all the way to the end.

For a long while, nobody said anything. They just waited, listening, wondering what was going to happen next. The authorities were sure to come, and Marolyn already had her story ready to be delivered.

"The silence is killin' me," muttered Margarette. "I'm about to go out there."

There had only been silence within the room. Beyond the doors was total chaos, and the commotion seemed to grow louder by the second.

"Ain't nothin' but trouble out there," Felicia said. She too wanted to go but knew it was best to stay put. Then, the startling ring of Shequita's cell phone commanded all of their attention in the room.

Teddy didn't even last long. His medicated infused brain put him back under before he could learn of his father's horrible death.

It was then agreed amongst them that Brandi should leave to go check out what was going on. She more than welcomed the opportunity to go investigate.

It wasn't a minute after Brandi left did Geno make his presence known in the room. The good man looked as disheveled as this whole situation was. And he didn't waste any time telling what he knew in regard to the demise of Timothy Anderson.

"He took down both cops like it wasn't no pressure to him. Somehow, he managed to get the drop on them during all the chaos," said Geno, a bulky man himself and another Army veteran. "He never made it outta the room before..." he paused uncomfortably.

"You don't even have to say it, Geno," Felicia replied and looked over at Marolyn. "May he rest in peace."

"He will now," nodded Tim's wife.

There was a moment of silence in the room.

Again, Shequita's cell phone rang, and this time, the call came all the way through. When she answered, Shequita listened for a second, sucked in a sharp breath of shock, and cried, "No! Ohmygod, no!" before her hand unconsciously reached for her heart.

That was when Avery rushed to catch his best friend's mother in his arms when she suddenly fainted.

And Teddy was still snoring.

Dead sleep.

"The phone," Margarette said instinctively just before it fell from Shequita's hand and hit the floor. She moved to pick it up just as the door opened, and Lenny Davis entered the room. The look on his face was all Avery needed to see to push Shequita off into Geno's care and step forward to confront the man.

"You trespassin' here, old man."

"Move outta my way, little boy." Lenny waved him off and stepped around him.

The side step was the move Avery was hoping for, and he took the opportunity. He hit Lenny Davis so hard in the jaw that the impact gave off a sickening cracking sound as he bounced off the wall and hit the floor with a heavy thud.

"Damn," was all Felicia could say.

Lenny Davis had walked into a den of wolves and was now suffering from his poor decision.

Chapter 19

The four of them moved through the shadows of the night like mercenaries.

Flip lived in a five-bedroom house on Hamilton Street, four houses down from where Shane lived. But Shane and his two cronies stayed back and let the real killas do what they did best. Surrounding Flip's house was a fence with a "Beware of Dog" sign posted up along the gate. Behind the house was a makeshift concrete platform slab that another fence circled around to house the ten dog kennels that were inside. Also occupying the backyard was a large portable steel building structure that Flip made into his mechanic shop and what was also a clubhouse.

And Twan had no trouble scaling over the front gate like he was jumping track and field hurdles. He moved silently and with the smoothness of a panther.

The others leapt over the gate in the same fashion, but their presence could have been heard, Cody in particular. He hadn't had time to strap his vest back on and was going in Rambo style, no shirt and pure fearlessness. The introduction of jumping into such a dangerous lifestyle had been one helluva mission.

Cody was just following the lead.

He was still learning.

"Two!" Twan signaled with a hand gesture, indicating that they should split up in two-men forces.

Money Mel nodded, and without faltering his momentum, him and Rod cut a sharp left along the side of the house. Together, Twan and Cody took the right route around the back of the house where the actual drive-by car from earlier was parked beside the steel building. The closer they got, they could hear the commotion going on inside the building.

At the scent of trouble, the pack of pit bulls inside the big dog cages nearby began to go berserk. That was all the motion Twan needed to charge harder so as not to allow Flip and the others to regroup in alarm before he made his grand entrance.

Cody watched with growing wonder as Twan accelerated all two hundred forty-five pounds of pure pressure of himself and suddenly rammed through the body that eventually appeared in the doorway of the building.

Blocka! Blocka!

Cody didn't know what else to do except shoot the person that Twan had literally ran over. He knew he couldn't risk him getting the ups on them whenever, or if he ever managed, to get back up.

Twan upped his tool and zeroed in on Flip, who was kneeling over Zed's bloody body lying on a tarp-covered pool table, tending to the gunshot wound that Zed took to his upper bicep.

"Ain't did nothin'!" Flip bellowed and raised his arms in surrender. "Don't shoot me, dawg!"

That was when Coba, a large rednose pit bull with vicious eyes and a head as big as a human's, suddenly rounded the corner of a tool cabinet. The dog looked like it weighed at least one hundred pounds solid. Coba looked up at Twan with murder in its eyes, and Twan sneered right back down at the dog.

Cody shot Coba dead in the face.

"No!" Flip cried out, and then Twan rushed him hard, gripping a hand around his throat and power-driving him into the floor. The impact caused Flip to bite his tongue and shed blood from it.

Without saying a word, Twan shoved the barrel of his Berretta into Flip's mouth, breaking some of his teeth in the process. *Boc! Boc! Boc! Boc!* Twan squeezed the trigger, dumping rounds into Flip's head as blood and gore splattered all up in his face.

By that time, Money Mel was holding Jay Baby under gunpoint, and Rod held Zed down against his will on top of the pool table.

"I wasn't even there when that shit went down," Jat Baby said from the bench he had been sitting on when the killas arrived. "That nigga did that shit. I was here the whole time."

"Bitch ass nigga! You a… bitch!" Zed exclaimed.

"Shut up, Zed!" Jay Baby snapped. "Me and Lank told you not to pull that move, and you did it anyway. Now you don' got these niggas on some fuck shit!"

Twan walked over to where Zed lay, blood all over the table and himself. "You killed my sista."

"And my daddy, nigga," snarled Cody as he stepped over next to Twan. "I saw you do it," he said. Images of the shooter hanging out of the car window with a TEC-9 flashed in his mental and made Cody place the gun against his forehead.

He then pulled the trigger with pleasure.

Click!

The gun was empty.

Instinctively, Twan took up the big hunting knife that Flip was apparently about to use to sear and pluck the bullet out of the gunshot wound. When Zed saw the knife, his eyes widened with fear.

"C'mon, Twan, man, I'm sorry…" Zed was cut short of begging for his life when the blade of the knife was driven into his right eye socket.

That shit made Cody cringe in instant shock as Zed froze briefly, grunted, and screamed so loud that it shook the building around them.

Twan withdrew the knife and repeatedly began to stab Zed in the mass space of his body: torso, stomach, ribcage. Every plunge of the blade created a sound so terrifying that exploded from Zed that it made Rod's own stomach cringe. The actual sound effects were the worst.

Blood splattered onto Cody in the process, but he dared not snatch his eyes away. This was killing to a whole other degree for him.

It was messy.

After killing Zed so mercilessly, Twan then turned his attention on Jay Baby. Jay Baby shivered in fear and pleaded for his life.

"Please don't kill me, dawg. I wasn't part of that shit. Lank told me not to get involved, and I didn't. I told them fools what was gon' happen," Jay Baby said in a flurry of words laden with fear at being killed like the others had.

"If I call Lank right now, he would say what you just said?" Money Mel replied.

"Hell yeah!" blurted Jay Baby.

"My own cousin would lie for me too," said Rod. Then he shot Jay Baby in the head. "And if Lank got a problem wit' that then he can come see me."

~   ~   ~

Kelvin Moore was a mountain of a man, fifty-five years old, with a fresh cut Boosie fade and a rigid demeanor. His jet-black eyes were like coal when he was annoyed, which was almost always. Kelvin had risen through the ranks of the Quincy Police Department through hard work, good planning, and the well earned respect of his predecessors. He was the chief of police now, and the chief was pissed off after having been awakened out of good sleep to come and see what the fuck was going on in his town.

There was a sudden and reverent silence among the group inside the room after his booming authority was delivered with his entrance. It was as if they were watching an eclipse or volcanic eruption.

But Felicia was the one who broke the silence and turned her glaring gaze upon the chief. "First off, I don't appreciate how you just gon' walk up in here and accuse us for whatever the fuck it is that brought your ass out here in the first place. This is a moment of grief for us, and the least you could do is show some fuckin respect, Chief."

"Or get the fuck out," added Avery. His hand was swollen from punching Lenny.

Chief Moore glared past the son and looked directly at the mother. "How dare you talk to me in that language and tone, Felicia. I am the law!"

"Fuck…" said Felicia before Shequita touched her arm and squeezed it soothingly.

"I appreciate your concern, Kelvin, but like my friend said, this is a very difficult time for us. The law does not stand in this room because no one did anythang wrong," said Shequita in that humbled tone of hers.

"Did nothin' wrong?" The big man reeled back in astonishment and said, "You sicced that boy on Lenny Davis and broke his jaw! That's not wrong?"

"That boy was protectin' his family," said Margarette.

"So, you're saying Lenny was the aggressor?"

Felicia shrugged.

And then he turned on Marolyn and looked at her with a grim expression. "And you," said the chief, "I know you was aware of what your husband did tonight. I should have you arrested for conspiracy to commit murder."

"My husband was a great man," she said.

"The man…"

"Get the fuck outta here!" Teddy's sudden explosion startled everybody in the room. He was now sitting up in the bed, and through the bloody bandages covering his ruined face, Teddy scowled and screamed. "Leave us alone! Get the fuck out!"

"Yeah," said Geno and rose up from where he had been sitting quietly. "It's time that you leave, man. You're upsettin' the atmosphere, and your presence is no longer needed here." He stood firm before the other man.

"Didn't need it from the get-go," muttered Avery.

Right then, Detective Raymond Williams entered the room, and it was all the chief could do not to blow up at him too.

"You people are a disgrace to our community," Chief Moore replied before heading for the door and shoving Ray out of the way.

Ray clenched his fist. "Chief," he hissed.

The big man said, "This ain't the last of me!" and stormed out of the door at once. Him being his superior didn't matter to Ray, and he wanted so badly to follow him out the door and check him on the disrespect.

"Pussy nigga," Avery spewed madly.

The tension in the air was thick, and Ray contemplated on how he should deliver the additional bad news.

"We already know what happened, Ray," Margarette said as though having just read his mind.

"Know what?"

"About what went down at Tami's house. She already called and told us," said Shequita.

"Was you there?" Geno asked. "I mean, did you see... It was horrible, I know." He shook his head sadly and moved back over to the chair he had been sitting in a minute earlier.

Grudgingly, Ray told them his version of the situation, and it created suffering grief in the hearts of those in the room with him.

"Did you see Cody?" asked Avery.

"Naw," answered the detective. "But he is wanted for questioning on certain matters that can't be overlooked."

"Certain mattress such as what?"

"Participatin' in the murders of a few people who lost their lives tonight," he said somberly.

"Cody?" Avery said in disbelief. "Nah, man. You gotta be mistaking him for somebody else."

"I wish I was, Avery."

"Then what're you gonna do about it, Ray?" Felicia said and stared the man dead in his eye. "You gon' stand up and protect your son, or you gon' let them crackers bury him in the system too?"

"Son?" Avery looked at his mother. "What?"

Detective Raymond Williams stared at Felicia unblinkingly, his heart rate accelerating with the sudden fear and surprise that her words caused him.

She knows, he thought dreadfully. Tami had told her he was Cody's real father.

"Don't look so surprised, Ray." This came from Shequita, and her gaze was intense. "What're you gonna do?"

All of a sudden, he felt trapped.

Ray was speechless.

And there was only one thing he could do.

He ran.

Chapter 20

"Av?"

Avery turned at the stern tone of his mother's voice calling out to him.

"Go get him," said Felicia. Now she was siccing her son on somebody. And Avery didn't even hesitate bounding for the door and pursuing the fleeing detective.

Wherever Raymond Williams thought he was going to escape the truth of who he was, his attempt would be deemed futile. He was still Cody's father, and there wasn't a damn thing he could change about that. It was niggas like him that made sistas not want to fuck with a Black man.

Due to the panic the fire alarm had caused, all kinds of people had been rushed out of the hospital. Then the gunshots created total pandemonium. There were cops prowling all over the place. Droves of people were still standing outside out front and at the back entrances of the building. Only a trickle of residents were being wheeled back in by clinical staff while a murder scene was being investigated.

The detective was bypassing everybody who dared to stop him or shoved past them all in the same motion. He was not running, but his retreat was long stretched in strides and of a hurried manner.

He looked like a man on a mission.

Twice, Avery had marched past a curious cop who wanted to know what he was up to. He just kept it moving in the direction in which Detective Raymond Williams had taken at a head start before him. Avery cleared the front entrance where a bunch of people stood, spectating and scared to go back inside for fear of something happening.

That was when Avery felt himself being shoved off balance and bumping into a middle aged female. Instinctively, he grabbed a hold of her to prevent her from falling over. Then, he turned toward the person who caused the problem and saw three grim faces staring back at him. One of those faces was someone Avery knew, and his name was Trent, the big brother of Breanna, the girl who him and his twin beat up at the rec center. The other two, Avery didn't have a clue who they were, but they obviously were on Trent's side.

"Wanna try that shit again now that I'm facing you?" Avery sneered at the three boys.

Trent Copeland, who was about thirty pounds less than Avery and two inches shorter, looked terrible for an eighteen-year-old. The partying and hard drugs would do that to you, and Avery knew without a shadow of a doubt that Breanna's brother was no match for him.

That was why the guy to his left stepped forward, bigger and broader, fearlessness sparkling in his dark eyes. "I'll beat your ass to sleep, lil boy!" he said.

Avery smirked at the challenge. But that was before he saw the black Impala SS starting up its engine several yards to his left. Ray. He was about to leave. Weighing his options quickly, Avery beat it for the car just as it was slowly pulling away. But that didn't stop him from snatching open the passenger door and sliding into the seat next to the startled detective.

Another smirk crossed Avery's face as he looked at the man beside him. Ray's instinct was to go for his gun, but then he didn't.

"You can't run from the truth, Ray," he said.

"Get out my damn car," Ray shot back. "Now!"

"You don't want me to do that, dawg." There was a threat hidden in that statement that Ray knew could mean trouble for him that he didn't need right now. Avery knew what he was doing, then he said, "All this time, you've been Cody's old man and never once said anythang? You know how much shit my brotha had to go through growin' up?"

For a long minute, the man didn't say anything. Then, when he did, the words came out in a strain. "It's complicated, Avery," he said.

"Is that what you gon' tell my brotha?"

With a shake of his head, Raymond Williams preceded on and pulled the car into traffic. Having to explain himself to Avery was the last thing he wanted. But then again, if he could convince Cody's childhood friend that regardless of the situation, he meant well, then maybe Avery could somehow be of help softening the blow.

"How did that shit even happen anyway?" asked Avery, rubbing his sore hand.

"C'mon, son. You know how those thangs are done," Rau replied. "You ain't green."

"You talkin' about sex? I'm not talkin' bout that. What I meant is how you and Aunt Tami clicked? She don't even like the police!" said Avery.

"You know we all went to school together? Me, your mama, Tami, Felicia, and Lenny?"

"So, what?"

"Tami was real wild back in the day. She was the most audacious person I know." Then, Ray went on to tell him how after they all graduated, he enlisted to the U.S. Marines. He came home after four years and decided to join the police academy. It was during a traffic stop after he spotted a Dodge Chrysler swerving down High Bridge Road that he stopped the car, and then there was Tami, still pretty as ever and apparently wild by the nature of her predicament.

"She was pissy drunk, and the open container of Budweiser was in the passenger seat beside her. She had drank a whole twelve pack and could barely say a straight sentence without slurrin'. I shoulda took her ass straight to the drunk tank at the station," said Ray with regret that he didn't.

"Why didn't you?" asked Avery. They were just riding around aimlessly as they talked.

"Because she was Tami," he said. "She was a childhood friend, like you, Teddy, and Cody," added Ray.

"They're my brothas," corrected Avery. "Anyway, what did you do after that?"

"I put her in the back of my squad car and took her home. By this time, I didn't know her and Corey was messin' around. He was wherever he was while his woman was out there ridin around pissy drunk, tryna numb her pain."

"Her pain?" Avery looked at him sideways.

Tami had just learned that her mother, Ella Mae Smith, died after her year-long fight with cancer. The stubborn woman had waited too long to seek medical treatment after she found two lumps in her private area. Ella fought the cancer head on and died right there in her kitchen at home where Tami had found her."

The very same kitchen that Alisha had lost her life in tonight as well.

"I checked on her from time to time after that," said Ray with earnest. "Then, a week later, my own parents was out on a fishin' expedition at Lake Jackson when they found their boat overturned in the lake."

"What?" said Avery, surprised.

Ray nodded. "I lost both of my parents that day. The day after I proposed to my then fiancée. Well, to make a long story short, Tami was there to lend her support. We leaned on one another for strength, and one thang led to another. Two months later, I get a call from Tami tellin' me that she was pregnant." He frowned at the memory.

"And you didn't believe her." Avery said this as he stared out his side window.

"I believed her the moment she said it."

Avery glanced his way. Now there was the part that the detective knew would matter the most in this whole matter.

"But I couldn't accept that responsibility at that moment, Avery. I already had so much on my plate. We both understood the severity of the situation, and havin' an abortion was outta the question. I was engaged to my fiancée, I had just transitioned to becoming a detective and was investigating my parents' death, plus it wasn't safe for her and the baby wit' the enemies I'd created behind the badge. So, Tami and I agreed on an arrangement where I still could help her provide for Cody when needed. And I've been doing that since the day he came into this world." Detective Williams turned onto a neighborhood street in the Friendship area and brought the car to a stop in front of a nice, white picket fence house.

Quietly, Avery dwelled on the matter, and he believed everything the man had said. But he understood his plight, and getting Tami pregnant wasn't what either expected. It was something that came with their intimacy, the way in how they needed each other, all the while making what friendship they had more complicated.

And Cody wasn't going to go for that. Cody needed a true father in his life, and he wasn't too distracted to really focus on family.

The man was everything his own father had been to him when he was growing up.

Poor excuse for a man.

To Avery, his brotha from another mother had been cheated out of a better life that he could have had if only Ray had stepped up and fathered his son.

"I had so many odds stacked against me to be the father I knew Cody needed," said the detective as if reading Avery's added thoughts.

"So, what'cha gon' do now, Ray?" Avery repeated the million-dollar question that sent the man running the first time back at the hospital.

With a deep breath, Ray said, "I have no other choice but to do what needs to be done, Av."

"And what's that?"

Ray looked at him. "I'm gon' go out there and save my damn son," he said. "Be right back." He opened the door and got out the car.

Having been caught up in his own thoughts, Avery didn't realize that Ray had taken him to his house. He watched as Cody's real biological father let himself in the gate and then through the front door of the house he shared with his wife and daughter.

And still, Avery was totally oblivious to the threat that had been lurking behind him the whole time.

He was about to have a rude awakening.

The elemental of surprise.

The beginning...

~   ~   ~

The foul taste and the watering in his mouth was what alerted Cody of what was about to happen. He drew a shaky breath, dropped his head between his legs, and vomited all over the floor of the backseat.

"Shit!" Rod, who was sitting in the back next to him, pushed himself up against the door. "This lil muthafucker is throwin' up back here!" he said.

Without saying a word, Twan and Money Mel both reached over to wind their windows down. Cody needed some fresh air, and they damn sure didn't want to be stuck having to smell his vomit.

When he was done, his eyes stinging, his stomach knotted up and queasy, Cody took another deep breath and fell back against the seat and closed his eyes.

"You good, Young C?" asked Twan.

Cody didn't reply.

They had just finished killing Flip and the others, and it was all Cody could think about. From what he had to do to Tysheed and then watching Twan do what he did to Zed, his digestive system didn't agree with it all and the pressure exploded.

"Now here comes the nightmares," said Twan.

"I told him that already," Money Mel spoke up. "He knows that shit comin' for his ass too."

"Fuck both of y'all!" Cody said, grateful that he couldn't actually see what he'd thrown up. He knew earlier he had swallowed some of Tysheed's blood and was banking on that being what made him vomit.

"It's time to switch cars anyway." Rod announced and informed them that Brian "Yak" Donaldson had two more cars for them at their disposal. He then gave Money Mel the location where to go to retrieve one of the stolen cars. "And we gotta torch this one while we at it," he said before lighting up a Black&Mild cigar.

Ten minutes later, they switched cars and hopped into a gray Mercury that Yak had left parked on the back road behind the old projects. Twan accepted the task of stuffing a cloth he'd found in the trunk into the input of the gas tank and setting flame to it. They weren't even a quarter mile away before the car exploded and shattered the night's silence.

Meanwhile, Sand was calling and delivering the good news about Menace. She had performed a satisfactory surgery, and Menace was now set up in one of the bedrooms that Meesha prepared for him.

"That reminds me," said Twan after he hung up with Sand, "I gotta tell Ms. Connie."

"Who is that?" asked Cody.

She was Dale's loving grandmother, who he had committed his love and life to caring for. His biological mother was in prison serving twenty-five years for killing another woman about playing with her money. Dale was twelve years old when his mother left, and it was his grandmother who took him in and raised him.

Hearing Twan tell his story made Cody think about Teddy and how he could have died as well. One of his wounds was three inches from the jugular vein. So close. If Teddy had died, Cody didn't know what he would do. So, he could pretty much sympathize and understand how Twan must feel right now. Too much killing and not enough vengeance.

"You live by the gun, you die by the gun," muttered Money Mel. "I guess we all will find out one day."

Stomach still queasy, Cody sat in the back quietly as they rode to Shaw Quarters turf. The Mercury parked in front of a red brick house on the same corner of the neighborhood park.

Together, Rod and Twan got out and trudged up to the front door of the house.

"You sure you a'ight, lil brah?" said Money Mel as he glanced back at Cody.

"Nothin' ain't never gon' be a'ight again, Mel. So please stop askin' me that shit," Cody told him.

That was a response Money Mel didn't expect from him. When he opened his mouth to say something, he was interrupted by the ringing of his cell phone.

"Mama," Money Mel said once he recognized her number on the screen. Then, a premonition overwhelmed him as he swallowed nervously and answered the phone. "What's going on, Mama?" he answered.

From the backseat, Cody heard Money Mel's sharp intake of breath, then he said something about his father, then another sound came from him that Cody knew all too well. The news he was receiving wasn't good, and Cody could sense the sadness wafting from him.

Cody decided to give him his privacy to grieve and got out the car.

138

Then, there was the unmistakable cry in the wind that resounded from the front door of the house. Cody turned just in time to see the old lady fall into Twan's arms in the doorway. Then, him and Rod assisted Connie Jones back inside the comforts of her home. Then, Cody felt something awaken his heart.

Everybody was sad right now.

Many hearts had been broken tonight.

And it wasn't over.

There was more blood to shed.

More blood indeed.

Chapter 21

Her name was Von, and she was on a mission to get some straightenin'. Vontoria Roberts was the daughter of Vincent Roberts, a man who had suffered greatly tonight after being stabbed in the eye with a Bic ink pen. The thrust had also pierced his brain and disrupted some inner nerve system. Right now, Vincent Roberts was wishing that he'd never messed with Avery.

So, that was why Von was coming. She wanted to avenge her father's honor and at the same time prove to him that no matter what he thought of her lifestyle, she would still always be there for him.

Von was twenty-one years old, but the differences between her and her father began when she was fifteen, and he walked in on her eating the pussy of Simone Leacock, the woman he himself wanted a piece of but could never get. It was then that Von confessed to her father that she was into girls.

But what took the cake was when her father went about plundering through her bedroom closet and dresser drawers one day while she was attending school and found her hustle stash. Vincent hit the fuckin' roof, marched right up to her school, snatched her out of her class, brought her home, and after rebuking her over what he found in her room, he kicked her out of his house. As for her mother, Sonya, by the time she got home that afternoon, the damage was already done.

Von was already gone.

And straight to the trap house she went where her mentor, Big Dot, took her in and showed her the way of life. By the time Sonya found her, Von was in too deep to even care about coming back home. Sonya Roberts literally stayed right there in the trap house until Von sold her last pack and thought she could convince her then. Von wasn't hearing her, plus the money was looking too good, and she loved the freedom she had to live how she saw fit to her liking. She made that clear to her mother, and Sonya left and never came back.

Von cried that day for the last time. Her and her mother were tight, more like sisters than mother and daughter, and it hurt Von that she had caused her mother pain.

Over the years, Von had transitioned from petty hustler to a young boss player in the game. She now owned a nail shop, a weed dispensary, and controlled her own booming trap houses in Tallahassee. Von had become quite successful in her endeavors and committing herself to a beautiful Dominican and Black queen named Reyzyne, who she was paying her way through college to study law. Her and Reyzyne were admired by many, and it was already known that Von would kill about her bitch, for it had already been done.

Gradually, Von's parents had come to accept her decision now that she was grown and successful, but they obviously didn't respect it either. Her father, being the proud and stubborn man that he was, still didn't allow her to step foot in his house. When she called to check up on them, the man would just hand the phone over to his wife. No matter what Von did or said, she could never get through to her father.

She had burned him eternally.

Losing her to the streets was all Vincent Roberts could take, and it killed him to let her go.

His only child was dead to him.

She was a disgrace.

But tonight, she was about to prove otherwise. All Von needed was a name, and when she got it, she set off to go get her man.

Avery Battles lived in Quincy, Florida, which was about eighty miles from Tallahassee. Von frequented the small town often to check in on a few associates over in the Havana area, even out in East Quincy where her Auntie Pooh lived. She was no stranger to Gadsden County, and to be honest, she had even considered moving out that way to get away from the big city for a change. Despite her high maintenance and quality, Von would love to explore her country roots because her parents both came from Valdosta, Georgia, and that southern country life was in her blood, not that city life where too many rules applied.

But overall, Von was a gangsta, and she would forever be a gangsta, and nobody could tell her different. There was no place on Earth that she felt she couldn't go, and her respect would be due to her. So, if Daddy didn't respect her now, he damn well was going to respect her later after she got ahold of Avery once and for all.

"It says here on Facebook that a reported twelve murders have been committed in the last twenty-four hours down in Quincy," said Daisy. This was Von's righthand man, another thoroughbred bitch whose body count extended over the one in which she had just read about on social media on her iPhone.

"Told you these country ass niggas don't fuck off 'round that way," added Remmy, the driver of the SUV that they were all riding in for this mission.

"Which means it's hot where we going, y'all, so we gotta stay on point at all times. We move accordingly; we don' did this shit before. I just hope this lil nigga don't make me chase his ass all 'round this muthafucker," said Von from the front passenger seat as she caressed her Glock .23 while pulling on a nice blunt of Runtz weed.

They were about a mile away from entering Quincy's territory. Von was anxious to get to where she was going and be done with it. But little did she know the hell she was about to go through.

Her Quincy contact was a business associate that went by the name of Mane, who lived in the Hill Side area in town. Whatever was going on in his town, he hadn't bothered to tell her. Von would have thought he would have at least disclosed to her some shit was already going down there.

Her initial contact had been Bizkit, but for some reason, the nigga wasn't answering his phone. She knew if it had been him, he would have given her the lowdown on whatever was going on in his neck of the woods. Bizkit was official, and she had mad love for him. They had made a lot of good money together.

When they finally arrived in town, Remmy was directed to Twenty-Four, which was the 24-Hour Kelly Jr. store on Pat Thomas Parkway that sat just in the heart of Quincy. This was the main community store and gas station that had become a legend over the years for its memorable occasions and events. From being a murder scene to being robbed, a get together spot after high school football games to a hangout spot for the winos and gangstas alike, Twenty-Four was a place where everything got done.

Last Von heard, a bitch got shot in both of her knees after the club one night. It happened right there in the parking lot in front of everybody. That was months ago, just after Von left back for Tallahassee after attending a Bobby Fishscale concert at Club V-12. Now there she was, back on the scene and hoping like hell no shit popped off before she got her man.

When they pulled up at the spot, Von called Mane to inform him of her arrival.

"I'll be there in a minute," said Mane in a rush of words as if he was running out of patience.

"And Mane," Von replied evenly, "it's a lot of smoke in the air, and you didn't bother to tell me that I was walkin' into a warzone?"

"About that, my nigga," said Mane, "we'll talk when I see you in a minute. I got this lil' ho wit' me, and I'm bout to bust all in her throat. Later!"

At the sound of the phone being disconnected on the other end, Von frowned and shook her head warily. She willed herself to remain calm, knowing Mane wasn't even worth killin' for testing her patience.

"So now we wait on this nigga," Von muttered and took another pull from her blunt.

"Okay. While we wait, I might as well go in there and grab a few thangs," Daisy replied, then she glanced up at Von and asked, "You want somethin'?"

What Von wanted was to find Avery and do his little ass dirty. She still wasn't sure whether she should kill him or leave him permanently impaired like he had done her father.

Daddy will never see outta that eye again, thought Von with great vengeance.

Yeah, Avery would have to die for that. Plus, she was going to take both of his eyes as well. Feed them to her tabby cat, Bugz. Tonight, she would make an example out of Avery to never fuck with her family.

"You know what I like, Dee," she said to Daisy, and Daisy, after asking Remmy what he wanted, got out along with Remmy, who said he had to piss like a racehorse.

Von was left in the truck alone.

To her wicked thoughts.

~   ~   ~

Speaking of the devil, Avery was growing restless just sitting in the detective's car out front. Too much shit was going on out there while he sat there doing nothing.

144

To busy himself doing something, Avery reached to open the glove compartment. And that was where he found the gun, a semiautomatic handgun still secured in what appeared to be an ankle holster of some kind. Avery unclasped the gun and pulled it out.

Uncle Moby had shown him and Ava a thang or two about gun control and how to use it to their benefit. Uncle Moby was a retired gangsta and now an avid hunter, and the man knew his way around guns like he knew his own kinfolk. Avery was a fast learner and did his uncle proud.

Dropping the clip to check the magazine count, Avery slapped it back in and marveled over the gun. It was a small, compact piece that seemed to fit well in his hand as though it was meant to be.

Then, suddenly, the passenger door was snatched open by some unseen force. Avery turned in its direction and was instantly knocked sideways from a vicious blow to his face. Then, all of a sudden, he felt two pairs of hands grab him and pull him out the car. He was then dragged across the curb onto the concrete sidewalk where a series of blows rained down on him. One was a kick to the face that made Avery cry out in pain and sudden fear.

He was being jumped by three guys.

"Talk that slick shit now, nigga!" one of them said before he was kicked in the back of the head, and it dazed him afterwards.

When Avery risked a look to see who his assailants were, he was surprised to see Trent just before another kick landed near his kidney side. The impact caused him to really double over in agony.

Being jumped before wasn't ever this bad. Avery had been caught totally off guard. He didn't have time to set up a defense strategy this time.

But then, he remembered the gun, which was still clutched tightly in his hand.

The three attackers couldn't have seen the gun or else it would have brought Avery enough time to get himself right. That was their mistake. Now he must take advantage of the opportunity.

No sooner did the thought occur did one of the attackers somehow locate a brick during the beat down and retrieve it. Then, he smashed it down onto the side of Avery's face. This time, Avery screamed in panic and pain when he felt two of his teeth cave in from the blow of the brick. Tasting blood in his mouth, Avery mustered up the raging strength he had and forced himself up off the ground. In doing so, he upped the gun and shot one of his assailants in the face. Then, he swung the gun at Trent and squeezed the trigger, putting two slugs in his body. Trent did the two-step dance before his body hit the ground.

The third one took off running for his life as Avery dumped three shots after him. He missed and chased after him.

By this time, Ray was bounding out the front door of the house with his pistol in hand, ready to defend his family and authorize legal force.

The one who Avery was chasing after was the very same one who stepped to him at the hospital. He wasn't so tough after all now. Avery lifted the gun and sent another two rounds his way.

Missed again.

Then, Avery felt a sharp pain in his rib cage area that made him stop running. He bent forward at the knee and grabbed his side. Suddenly, it hurt when he breathed. Dizziness took over him, and the next thing he knew, Avery was down on his knees in the middle of the street.

He couldn't breathe.

It hurt.

"Av?" Ray came up behind him and rested a hand upon his shoulder. He sensed Avery was injured and knelt down next to him. "What's wrong, son? Where are you hurtin'?" he asked.

"My ribs," cried Avery.

With the ease of a caring man, Ray removed the gun from Avery's possession and tucked it away into his coat pocket. Then, he helped Avery stand up and said, "Let's get you in the house."

Slowly but surely, they made it back to the house without further incident. In passing, Avery looked at the two bodies laid out on the ground and feared the repercussions of that situation. At the front door of the house stood Ray's wife, Latrice, who reached to assist her man in helping Avery inside.

"I got him, Ray. Okay?" said Latrice, a pretty, petite, yellow bone woman in her mid-forties. "You go do your job outside, honey. Since that seems more important than your family."

When Ray detected the iciness in her tone, he was ready to confront her on it, but then he looked up and saw Rayneshia. His daughter was standing in the living room doorway with a scared look in her eyes. He sighed and turned away, back for the door, refusing to allow his own personal defaults to complicate things further than it already had.

"Easy now, I got'chu!" Latrice had helped Avery down onto a padded bench parked in the den area of her beautiful home. "Now tell me where the pain is?"

Rayneshia followed them inside quietly.

It wasn't easy, but Avery told her where so much pain was traveling through his body. He was hurting all over. Then, Latrice ordered Rayneshia to go fetch her the necessary items she needed to care for his injuries. He was really going through it.

Silent tears streamed down Avery's face as he struggled to breathe while fighting against the pain.

Latrice said, "It's gon' be alright, sweetie. Just remain strong and let me take care of you."

Returning with the items requested, Rayneshia assisted her mother with removing Avery's shirt and began the process of tending to his wounds.

Avery's face was swollen badly, as if his jaw was broken, but it wasn't. He could still talk, but it was a painful mission to do so.

After his wounds were tended to, Avery was led to the family guest room and left there to rest while they watched over him.

"If it ain't one thang, it's another around this damn house." Latrice expressed her frustration and left the room in a funk.

"She mad at me?" whispered Avery.

"No." Rayneshia touched his cheek tenderly. "She's just scared, Avery, that's all."

Looking up into her eyes, Avery became lost in the depths of her hazel gaze. He'd momentarily forgotten all about the pain and discomfort and the two bodies he left stretched out front of the house. The beautiful creature before him was mesmerizing.

"What?" Rayneshia spoke up again as her piercing hazel brown eyes captured him at his most vulnerable.

Snatched out of his trance, Avery had to remind himself that this was Cody's sister.

Rayneshia was eighteen years old, a freshman at FAMU College, majoring in business marketing, smart and very academic, but you couldn't deny the hidden mischief in her eyes. Only one who was of the same caliber could tell the difference. And Avery knew that this good girl that her parents thought she was was far from the truth.

"They gon' take me to jail for what I did," he replied.

"I don't think so, Avery."

He looked up at her questioningly. "Huh?"

From somewhere beyond the bedroom door, Latrice called out for her daughter. She gave Avery another lasting gaze and hurried out the room.

With a discomforting groan, Avery shifted his body beneath the comforter Rayneshia had laid over him. He glanced up at the nightstand at the clock. It was 2:20 a.m., and unfortunately, the night was still young.

And dangerous.

Avery couldn't believe he had killed Trent and whoever it was that was with him. He didn't even feel bad about it either. His only concern was going back to jail. The little couple hours he was being held in the Leon County Jail was treacherous, trapped in the holding cage with two transgenders, a redneck dopehead, and three drunks. The only toilet available didn't work and was overflown with piss and shit. Vomit from one of the dope-sick drunks was all over the floor. Hell no!

Avery would rather go on the run than be placed in another situation like that.

The emergency sirens filled the night as the calvary made their presence known. Avery braced himself for the fate his decision would deliver him. Once they saw the bodies and Ray told his colleagues what he did, there was no doubt in Avery's mind what would happen next.

"Not t'night," he grumbled fitfully.

Avery eased himself out of bed and over to the door and locked it. Then, he carried his painful body over to the window and unlocked it. He then, with what little strength he could muster up, lifted the window and glanced back at the secured bedroom door.

"Not t'night," he repeated. "Not me."

Chapter 22

Lil Earl watched from the back door of the house as Lank exited from the shop where yet another murder scene lay. You couldn't read the look on Lank's face due to the shadows of the night, but it was not to be mistaken. There was a murderous gaze there. He had just viewed the dead body of his little cousin and that of his crew. No one was spared. Even the dog had taken a slug to the head.

Standing just beyond Lil Earl's shoulder was Mercedes, her face a mask of dark fear and worry. She was inside, lounging in a nice, hot bubble bath, after being thoroughly dicked down by Flip. Then, his homies came beating the door down, screaming that Zed had been shot. Flip summoned them to the back in the shop, which was also their hangout spot. Then, fifteen minutes later, Mercedes heard gunshots out back and damn near drowned in the tub.

Scared out of her mind, Mercedes got out and rushed across the hall to the bedroom she shared with her man, Flip. There she armed herself with one of the guns he kept hidden around the house just in case something serious came up and he needed some ready protection. Mercedes locked herself in the room and waited, listening, watching through the window outside within the dark room.

And that was when she saw Twan, Rod, and Money Mel, the three niggas she did know, run through the door of the shop out back with some other young dude. It turned out that same young dude was Cody Williams, which Lil Earl had shared with her after she called him when the coast was clear.

Mercedes dared not leave the room until Lil Earl came knocking twenty minutes later.

This was her cousin, Yvonnie's man, and Mercedes knew Jay Baby was one of his little homies and that he was Lank's little cousin. So, she hit Lil Earl up and told him what she knew. He showed up by himself and went out back to investigate. Then, he phoned Lank with the bad news.

When Lank showed up, he did so with another relative of his by the name of Rontay. Rontay exited the shop after Lank, carrying a Mac-11 assault rifle in his possession. Both of them came strapped with heavy artillery in case shit got drastic.

Shis had gotten drastic for damn sure.

Jay Baby was dead.

"So, how you wanna do this, my nigga?" Lil Earl replied after allowing Lank and Rontay to slide past him into the house.

Lank didn't reply. He walked through the house toward the front. Now his facial expression was clear as day, and Lil Earl thought he looked more surprised than hurt or mad about what happened.

"He went against what I told him," said Lank once he made it up front and took a seat upon the black, leather sofa in the big living room.

"I see that." Lil Earl was present when Zed and Jay Baby called and expressed their concerns regarding Tysheed's beef with Cody and then his murder back over at the Pit tonight.

Zed was more adamant about seeking vengeance on Cody than Jay Baby was. When Lank gave the call to stay out the way, Jay Baby promised him that he would. Now he was dead, and Lank was being forced to deal with the bullshit.

Lank already knew what they were getting themselves into being crossed by Cody. He had a team of killers behind him, and the young nigga was hungry for blood. Especially after witnessing what he did tonight at the Pit, Lank knew his little cousin wasn't ready for that type of trouble.

"So, we let that shit slide or what? You know I'm down wit' whateva you down wit," said Lil Earl.

"Ain't lettin' shit slide, my nigga. Them niggas killed our own flesh and blood. Let what slide?!" Rontay was heated, but he was also responding out of emotions rather than common sense.

Mercedes said, "They murdered my man!"

"I told them fools to let that shit go!" Lank growled and shook his head. "Told them!"

"What the play is, cuz?" Rontay replied.

Lank just shook his head wearily.

"This nigga don' bitched up now!" sneered Rontay. "You scared now? Cuz, you a pussy! Real talk," he said.

Suddenly, Lank shot up to his feet and put himself in Rontay's face. Lil Earl stepped back cautiously, knowing how very dangerous Lank could get when disrespected.

"Cuz," snarled Lank in his cousin's face, "disrespect me like that again and I'll crush your fuckin' face, nigga."

"You'll blow up at me though?" Rontay shook his head wearily and said, "You'll fight me but not them niggas who killed Jay?!"

Lank continued to glare at him.

"And you expect me to respect that bullshit? To charge it to the game? Fuck that, cuz. I'm all in."

"Remember what happened to Two Head?"

Rontay was about to turn around and leave when the question gave him reason to pause.

"What that gotta do wit' this shit, Lank?"

Lank said, "Remember you told Two Head not to go out there and rob Rodney for them pounds of weed? And he did it anyway and Rodney killed his ass?"

"Why you bringing that shit up, cuz?"

"Because it's the same thang."

"It's not the same."

152

"Yes, it is! Two Head was your main man, and Rodney was your dawg too. You told Two Head what that nigga was gon' do if he took them pounds. And what did you do about that shit, cuz? Nothin'."

"That's different, cuz, and you know it. Jay Baby was family," said Rontay.

"And Two Head wasn't?"

To question whether Two Head was family or not would be an overwhelming process because Rontay and him had come from the sandbox together, and Rodney wasn't that far along after that. They were all friends coming up in the ghetto, then Two Head and Rodney bumped heads over some bullshit that could've been avoided. When Two Head saw the opportunity to hurt Rodney's pockets, he robbed him, and Rodney came back and killed him later.

And Rontay decided not to avenge Two Head's death because 1) He told Two Head not to do it and the consequences he would face, and 2) Rodney was also still considered a close friend as well.

"Wasn't Two Head family, cuz?" said Lank.

"He was," Rontay replied slowly.

"And what was Rodney?"

"He was family too."

"And so is Jay, and Twan, and Mel, and…" Lank was cut off by the sudden eruption of the dogs barking out back at whatever it was that alerted them.

Mercedes then heard the unmistakable sound of a car pulling up out front and hurried over to the living room window to look outside.

"Oh, no!" she said with great alarm.

"What?" said Rontay.

Mercedes gazed back at them, and the look of fear in her eyes was alarming. "The police out there," she said. With his Mac-11 in hand, Rontay rushed over to the window next. When he peered out through the curtains and saw the QPD cruiser, he went into a panic. When he then glanced back at his cousin, Lank saw the animalistic look in his eyes that only meant one thing.

Trouble was coming.

And somebody was about to die.

~   ~   ~

Mane pulled up in a black and red Dodge Charger, and Von shifted in her seat in anticipation when the text came through informing her that it was him.

Von then climbed over into the backseat so that Mane could ride shotgun. Plus, this gave her space and opportunity to put a bullet in the back of his head if she sensed foul play. He was a fine business associate, but this here was a whole other ballgame. Couldn't be too careful under such extreme circumstances.

Mane parked the Charger at the shoulder of the station building and got out. He was of average height, drippin' in jewels, and attired in Fendi wear, obviously not prepared for a murder mission as they were. But there was no doubt that Mane was strapped. Mane had a solid reputation of puttin' in work, and there was no sleepin' on niggas like him.

He swaggered over to the truck and got in.

"What it do, Daisy?" Mane slid into the seat next to Daisy, who was drinking from her bottle of Mountain Dew soda. She was Mane's crush. He thought Daisy was God's gift to a nigga like him. She wouldn't play on his affection though, only businesswise and straightforward, but Mane was still convinced he could win her over. "I was hopin' you was here t'night, beautiful," he said.

"I just bet you was," replied Daisy.

Remmy frowned in the backseat and made a hand signal of shootin' Mane in the head.

"What's going on around here, Mane?" Von spoke up, her tone firm and her attitude humbled.

"It's a war goin' on, Von. Niggas dyin' left and right t'night. Ya know Bizkit is dead?"

This astounded Von. "Really?"

He nodded and told them what he knew of the situation, and Von could only shake her head.

"Damn," she said. "I had hit him up first b'fore I called you. He never picked up. Damn. He prolly was already dead by then"

"Prolly," added Mane. "But what's really good though? When you called, you sounded upset. I'm feelin' the vibes. Who don' crossed you now?" Mane had been dealing with Von for a couple of years now, and he'd grown to understand some of her habits and personality. He knew she was more than a pretty face.

"Avery Battles," said Von.

"I don't think I know who that is."

"He's a young mutt."

"Oh. He's one of them," muttered Mane. "So, what's the deal wit' this little nigga?"

Von gave him the full lowdown on what happened to her father hours ago.

"Oh, shit." Mane didn't have to ask what was coming next for Avery. "A'ight. He can't be in the streets too much, or I'll already know or heard 'bout him. What else you can tell me about him?"

"I know he goes to East Gadsden High."

"And?"

"I got a picture of him too."

"Lemme see."

Von showed him. "His mama name is Felicia Bradwell. I tried lookin' her up online, but she don't even have a social media link. Not even in the phonebook. I need an address, Mane."

"I know Felicia," said Mane.

When he said this, Von heard the telltale of something questionable in his tone. He admitted that he knew Felicia, but there was something else behind those words.

"You more than just know her, huh, Mane?" Daisy replied curiously as she gazed at him.

"Avery is the boy twin," said Mane. "There's a sista too. Now it's all coming t'gether. They got into some shit t'gether at the rec center earlier t'day. That's prolly what led him to go to the Tent." That was when Mane retrieved his cell phone to show them the video that had been going viral lately. It was the video of first, Teddy getting sliced up by Tink Tink, then Avery and his twin sister coming to his rescue. The showdown was captured on video by some other young female named LeLe Mitchell whose ratings on social media had shot up from the video.

As she watched Avery in action, Von's heart began to race with adrenaline. "I want him."

Mane didn't reply.

"Where can we find him, Mane?" That was Remmy, and there was venom in his voice.

"In Pepper Hill."

"Pepper Hill. I know where that's at," said Daisy and started up the truck. "Where in Pepper Hill?" she wanted to know.

There was hesitation when Mane answered; both Von and Remmy looked at each other. "I'll show you where," he said.

Without a word spoken, Von drew her Beretta and unlocked the safety.

"Why do I feel like you don't really wanna show us where this lil' nigga lives?" said Remmy.

"Because I don't, nigga. I know these people. Felicia is good people; my little brother, Ty, is cool wit' her kids." Mane had an uncomfortable feeling that he had just put his own foot in his mouth. He personally didn't want to be involved in whatever Von had in mind to do to young Avery because he knew that would affect the rest of the crew, meaning Money Mel, and Money Mel was his nigga.

They were like family.

"Then how about this?" said Von. "You show us where they live, and we bring you back? You don't have to be personally involved. Plus, I'll give you a ten percent discount on our next shipment."

Reluctantly, Mane said, "Sounds like a plan."

Remmy reached over and tapped Von's leg, and she only just nodded her head in answer. That was all the indication he needed to pull out his gun and ready himself to take Mane's life.

Once they got the location, Mane died.

His hesitance was too alarming.

He was a liability.

But what they didn't know, but should know, was that Mane knew what their grave intentions were for him.

He was no dummy.

He was just waiting for the right moment.

Chapter 23

Avery was halfway out the window when out of nowhere, Rayneshia appeared right there on the scene. She was outside watching him struggle to make his painful escape from the whole situation.

"You are so pitiful, Avery," she said amusingly. "How I figured you was gonna do somethin' like this? Why are you tryna get away?"

Avery glanced down at her standing outside the bedroom window he was hanging halfway out of. The awkward position he was in had his ribs screaming in tremendous pain and agony.

"I can't stay here," he managed.

"Why?"

"Because," Avery said, "they gon' take me to jail."

"No."

"No?"

With her hands on her hips in that stubborn way that stubborn females do, Rayneshia looked up at him and said, "My daddy is takin' care of the situation. He's takin' full responsibility of what happened, Avery. Your involvement isn't being mentioned. You good. You don't have nothin' to worry about," she assured him.

"He's sayin' he did everythang?"

"Without question," she said and spotted the look of disbelief on his face. "Trust me, Avery. He knows what he is doing."

But Avery wanted out of the window anyway. Sensing this was what he wanted, Rayneshia stepped forward to help him down so as not to hurt himself further. Avery landed in her arms with severe agony, but with the smell of her body spray and the warmth of her embrace, he was once again taken aback by her essence.

"You okay?" she asked.

"No." Avery's right eye was swollen halfway shut, and he hated having her see him like this. He shrugged away from her and moved about the shadows toward the rear of the big house.

Rayneshia followed close behind him. She could tell he was still hurting despite the few Percocet tablets her mother had given him earlier. She watched as he walked aimlessly around the back until he spotted the swing set off the path leading from the back porch.

"This was yours?" He gestured toward the two swings.

"When I was a little girl, yeah."

"But you still use them," he said. "Maybe when you got a lot on your mind and wanna be alone to think." Avery didn't wait for her to answer and turned and eased down onto one of the still swings.

She took the one next to his. "How'd you know this one was my favorite swing, Avery?" Rayneshia grabbed ahold of the thick chain hanging about either side of her petite frame.

"I gotta find my friend, Cody," he said.

"Cody?"

He stared out into the night as it glowed about from the flashing of emergency lights on the other side of the house in front.

"Is Cody lost or something?"

"Yeah. Somethin' like that."

"How?"

Avery winced. "Somethin' happened earlier today, and we got separated. I ended up going to jail, and he was left out there to fend for himself, and now he's in trouble."

"What happened though?" she asked.

He told her how it all had begun up until where he sat at that very moment.

"But how did you get caught up wit' my daddy? You seemed to have left that part out, Avery. And why would he be risking his job to save you?" Rayneshia's curiosity was intensive, and for some reason, him leaving out that part of the matter made her worry a little.

"I don't wanna lie to you," Avery told her.

"Then tell me the truth, Avery."

"But that's not my place to tell it."

"Whether it's your place or not, Avery, I still deserve to know the truth. Whatever it is you and my daddy got going on, I really need to know. It could affect everythang we've accomplished together, and I need to know, so I can at least help figure this mess out. I'm scared." She cried openly in front of him. "I'm so scared I don't know what to do."

"Cody is your brotha, Rayneshia."

She went completely still. Rayneshia turned her teary eyes on Avery. "My brotha?"

And so he told her the truth.

When he was finished, Rayneshia was downright sobbing beside him. If Avery thought he was uncomfortable before, he was damn sure uneasy now, as he watched Rayneshia break down in front of him.

The back door opened. Latrice Williams stood in the open doorway, staring out after them. Her daughter's cries sent her hurrying in their direction. Now Avery was really uncomfortable as he anticipated the woman's nearing fury.

"What's the matter?" Latrice demanded of her daughter.

"Nothin', Mama. I'm okay," lied Rayneshia.

Latrice wasn't fooled by a long shot.

"She's just scared; that's all," said Avery, only to have the woman glare down on him.

"Your room door was locked when I went to check on you. I didn't see you leave the house. Did you get out

160

through the window? Why? You are supposed to be resting, young man!" she chastised Avery, and he knew there was nothing he could say to persuade her otherwise. "Let's go!" she replied.

"But she needs me…"

"Rayneshia can handle herself," said Latrice, glancing toward her only child and seeing that Rayneshia had gotten control of herself enough to speak up.

"Give us a minute, Mama, please? I'll bring him right in," Rayneshia replied.

"He shouldn't be outta bed in the first place."

"One minute, Mama."

The woman frowned. "Hurry up, you two. And you, Rayneshia, you should know better than anybody," she said and hurried back toward the house.

Neither one of them said one word until Latrice was back in the house with the door shut.

"Why do I feel like you just told her a lie?" Avery said, turning to look at Rayneshia.

"I did," she said.

"Why?"

"Because," she replied and climbed out of the seat of her favorite swing, "you're gonna show me where I can find my brotha, Cody."

"So, you believe me?" Avery was not surprised by this.

"Why would you lie to hurt me?" she said.

Then, she helped him up to his feet, and Avery asked her how they were going to pull this off.

"My friend, Kelli," she said.

Avery paused for a second. "Which Kelli?"

Without answering the question right off, Rayneshia took him by the hand and pulled him in the opposite direction of her house. She led him across the backyards of three neighboring homes through a short, dark path behind one house then came out onto the next street over. From there, it was the second house on their right where she led them. A minute later, Rayneshia was standing outside the bedroom window of a white and green stucco home with a screened patio.

She knocked on the window.

A light switched on in the room.

And Kelli Johnson's face appeared in the window, and it was all Avery could muster not to turn and run away that very second.

He swallowed nervously. "Oh. That Kelli."

Another minute later and all three of them were standing in the middle of Kelli's colorful bedroom.

"What is this I'm seeing right now? I thought you was gone to jail, boy," Kelli asked, her blue-colored braces shining like new teeth jewelry. Her statement caused Avery to look at her in quiet bewilderment.

"So, you know who he is already?" Rayneshia said this with amusement.

"Know him? Girl," Kelli shook her head, "this boy is my damn ex-boyfriend!" she said.

"Hmph." Rayneshia looked thoughtful for a moment. "Why haven't I heard about this, Kelli?"

"Because I didn't find it important enough to discuss."

"What did he do wrong?"

Kelli shot a sharp gaze at Avery. "It's not important. It wasn't then, and it damn sho' ain't now. Now," she replied more softly, "what happened to you?" Kelli reached up to touch his bruised face tenderly. "It hurts?"

Rayneshia regarded them both with soundless intrigue. It made her uneasy to see that Kelli indeed still had feelings for him. She wasn't sure why she cared so much; it wasn't like her and Avery were a couple.

"Gotta find my brotha, Kay-Kay," he said.

"Cody? Or Teddy? Oh. That's right. Teddy's in the hospital. So, you gotta be talkin' about Cody. What's up wit him? Where is he?" asked Kelli.

"I don't know. That's why I need to find him."

"Kay-Kay?" Rayneshia looked perturbed.

Kelli smirked. "That's my pet name that Av always called me when… Anyway, lemme put some clothes on, and we can go look for Cody." She too was eighteen years old but not as pretty as Rayneshia, but Kelli was smart and thorough. One thing Avery could say was that she had never done him wrong. It was his fault they had broken up two years ago. While Kelli wanted a stable relationship, Avery wanted to be there for his crew. That was during the time when Teddy lost his grandfather, and Avery lost interest in all but his brother's comfort.

He was always there for his brothers.

He was loyal.

But in a minute, that loyalty would be tested for more than he would have ever imagined.

~   ~   ~

Rod was left behind to assist Connie Jones in going to identify Dale's body. Then, he would meet up with the crew later and resume his thuggin' in the streets.

Meanwhile, Cody, Twan, and Money Mel were back in traffic and politicking on some gangsta shit.

Then, Po'Boy called to inform them on Lank's arrival at Flip's spot after Lil Earl showed up. That was why he chose to remain behind so that he could get a lead on Lank when he showed up. It was something that could not be denied. When Lank got wind of what went down, he was coming full speed ahead.

It was also determined that Mercedes had to be dealt with accordingly. By now, Lank and his crew knew who all was involved because of her.

Po'Boy crept back to the scene and was hiding in the shadows alongside the house. He was watching the interactions of them in the front room and assuming it was about to get bloody between Lank and Rontay. Then, the police showed up out front which made Po'Boy get somewhere other than there.

"So, Lank and 'em got somethin' on their minds," said Money Mel in the front seat behind the wheel of the Mercury now. "Let's go ahead and press play."

"Let's see how this shit turns out," Twan was referring to the police arrival at Flip's house. There was no telling how that would play out.

Cody was in the backseat quiet, thinking about the situation regarding Lank and what he had on his mind where Jay Baby's murder was concerned. He would kill him too if it came down to it.

"The way Po'Boy tell it, Lank don't really want no problems wit' us," said Money Mel.

"But Rontay does."

"Which might force Lank's hand to ride wit' him outta loyalty for their bloodline."

"Then they both will die together," said Cody.

"Straight like that," added Twan. His cell phone rang, and he retrieved it and saw it was his nigga, Souljah, calling him. This was his baby mama, Quanda's beloved godbrother. Souljah was a young fool but loyal to a fault. He was Twan's protege and the only little nigga he trusted to watch over his family.

"I'm back in town now, my nigga. Where you at? I got that paper for you," said Souljah.

He don't know about Alisha, thought Twan. It was going to fuck Souljah up when he found out that Alisha was dead. The shock hadn't really hit Twan yet, but when it finally did, it wasn't going to be pretty. Maybe that was why he was busying himself staying focused on street shit to prolong the shock of his sister's death when it hit him like a tidal wave. He wasn't ready for that yet.

"We can meet up," said Twan. "I'm in traffic right now as we speak."

They agreed on a location. Money Mel headed over in that direction to meet with Souljah.

"He's gonna flip the fuck out when I tell him."

"I know," Money Mel said.

The location was Twenty-Four where Souljah was inside purchasing blunts and a bag of Doritos when they pulled up on the scene.

"Po'Boy still ain't hit back yet," said Money Mel when he found a place to park the Mercury along the side of the station next to the adjoining laundromat service station.

"He's layin low right now, watchin' the movement," replied Twan humbly.

"But somethin' shoulda went down by now."

"We'll know soon, Mel. Patience."

Cody opened the door and got out the car.

Twan stared out after him and wondered what was on his mind.

"You know he's really scared, right?" Money Mel broke the momentary silence between them.

"Scared of disappointin' us," said Twan. "I wasn't there when that shit went down in the Pit, but I can pretty much grasp what he went through. It was either kill or be killed then, Mel, and now, it's kill kill kill so that he won't go through that shit again. You saw what he did back at Flip's crib? Young C didn't have to be told what to do. That first taste of power got him fienin' for more, but it scares him because he doesn't know how to control it."

"I pretty much told him the same thang."

"He gon' be a'ight, Mel."

"I hope so."

"For now, we just gotta keep him close so that he won't kill his muthafuckin' self!" chuckled Twan as he watched Souljah approach Cody outside the car after he beckoned him over.

Minutes later, they both were climbing into the back of the car. Cody carried with him a silent grimness so potent that it was hard for one not to see that he wasn't to be bothered.

Cody's presence reeked of danger now.

There was blood in his eyes.

"I'm hearing some wild shit going on out there in them trenches t'night."

"That all depends on who you're hearin' it from," said Money Mel.

Souljah looked from him to Twan then over at Cody and knew there was something very serious going on around him. "I heard it was that silly nigga, Wayne Jordan, just now," he said.

"Alisha is dead, Souljah," Twan told him.

"What?"

Twan didn't have to repeat himself.

"Dead? How... What!?" Souljah replied in absolute astonishment, then their silence made him turn to worry, then a wave of sadness exploded in him. He dropped his head for a long moment as he fought the urge to break something. No one said anything further and just let Souljah get past whatever it was that was going through him at that moment.

Money Mel's cell phone sounded off.

It was Po'Boy.

The shit had hit the fan in Lake Skillet.

Chapter 24

The cop at the front was someone that Mercedes knew from around the way. Her name was Amanda Turner, an older female in her late thirties, the daughter of a well-respected school principal and an army veteran father. When Mercedes opened the door and saw her there, she figured she could talk her way out of this like she'd done so many other times before.

"How ya doing, Officer?" She put her game face on.

"Got a call that gunshots were heard coming from this residence," said Officer Amanda Turner, her eyes sharp and attentive. "Know anythang about that?"

"I think there's been a misunderstandin', Officer. No gunshots coming from this house at all," she replied.

"Is there anybody else in the house?"

Mercedes hesitated. It was then that she spotted the woman's partner approaching from behind. This was a younger, white guy, tall and burly built, and seeing him only made matters more worrisome.

"Um. honestly, Officer, everythang's okay here," said Mercedes.

The female cop didn't look convinced.

The second cop didn't make his way for the front porch but scanned the perimeter surrounding the residence. Then came the barking of the dogs out back, which seemed to pique his interest. When he directed his attention in that direction, Mercedes damn near shit a brick.

"If everythang's okay, then you won't mind me and my colleague have a look around?" said Officer Turner, who reminded you of a younger Regina King but of a lighter skin complexion.

"I don't think that would be wise."

"Why not?"

"Because this isn't my house. My boyfriend, Flip, owns this house, and he's not home."

"Flip? Are you talkin' about Favion Dennis?"

At the mention of Flip's real name, Mercedes knew she was in for a surprise. Then, the cop stepped forward and pretty much forced Mercedes to step back out of her way to step over the threshold.

"You can't just barge your way in here!" objected Mercedes.

"Flip won't mind," she answered.

"No!"

Mercedes blocked her way, and the cop, he hand resting on the handle of her sidearm, gazed up at her with the intensity of a cornered leopard.

"You need to move out of my way."

"No."

The cop frowned. "Please don't make me..." She didn't finish her statement before rapid sounds of automatic gunshots rang out outside. Instinctively, she drew her service weapon and regarded Mercedes with hot suspicion.

Mercedes had a sick look on her face.

With the gun now pointed at Mercedes' chest, the officer reached for her shoulder radio to call in the code red to dispatch. Then, before she could get the first word out, Rontay spun from around the corner, into the foyer, with his Mac-11 ready.

"Don't do it," he warned her, leveling the assault rifle goon-style and scowling darkly at her. Rontay only needed one false move, and it was over.

"No, Rontay! You don't do it! Put the gun down." Officer Turner was standing directly in front of Mercedes, as her body was a shield between her and the big gun. "Put the gun down, Rontay!" she barked.

Mercedes didn't dare move for fear of causing herself to be gunned down.

"All you need to do is put your gun down, and I'll let you live. Don't make me do this shit," he said.

"Let me live? Really, Rontay? You'll kill your own cousin? Me?" said Officer Turner.

Cousin? thought Mercedes in astonishment.

"You ain't shit to me, Manda! You chose the other side over family. You just like them crackers you work for! You don't give a fuck about family!"

"I have a job to do, Rontay. Put the gun down. Please?"

"You a snake, bitch," he sneered.

"Manda?" another voice replied.

At the sound of her name being called, she stiffened and glanced over her shoulder behind her. When she saw Lank standing there with his gun in hand, Amanda felt her heart pound brutally with fear.

That was when Rontay made his move.

When Amanda heard his approach and turned back toward Rontay, he was already upon her, and the butt of his Mac-11 bashed her in the face with brutal force. At the same instant, her gun discharged with a shocking blast just as the bridge of her nose shattered on impact.

Rontay staggered backwards a few steps, looked down on himself, and saw the bullet hole in his stomach. "You fuckin' shot me!"

"Cuz, no!" Lank bellowed. He saw Rontay look back up at Amanda with that murderous glare and rushed in to him at once. He made it to Rontay before he could pull the trigger and kill Amanda. "C'mon, Rontay! We gotta get you outta here, cuz!"

Scared to death, Mercedes watched as Lank pressed the palm of his hand against his cousin's wound. Rontay screamed bloody murder, and together, they rushed out through the front door.

A car sat idling at the curb out front with Lil Earl behind the wheel. Lank snatched the rear door opened, and they climbed inside.

At the sound of screeching tires in the night, Mercedes turned her gaze on Officer Amanda Turner. The female cop looked to be in excruciating pain as she struggled to her feet. Her face was gushing blood profusely as she stumbled for the open front door.

Once outside, Amanda stumbled alongside of the house toward the back where her partner had gone. There she found the white cop sprawled out on the ground in front of the clubhouse. It appeared as though he had been shot multiple times. Dead as a doorknob.

"Oh, no," gasped Mercedes in horror.

Amanda, although she was in tremendous pain and agony, turned an evil look on Mercedes and was tempted to blow her fucking brains out.

~   ~   ~

There was a thick silence in the air within the SUV as they entered the Pepper Hill territory.

In the backseat, Von bounced her knee anxiously as Mane directed their way. Now she knew more than what she started off with in regard to Avery and where he came from. Mane was very knowledgeable in that aspect, being that he was familiar with what was going on.

"Up here on the left where that big white church at on the corner." Mane pointed up ahead as Daisy nodded her head in silent understanding.

Beside Von, at Mane's right, Remmy had materialized with ripcord wire of about four foot long. He passed it over to Von without actually telling her what she should do with it. It was so like Remmy to have some type of weaponry that was not of the average choice for a street dude. He was a certified killer, and the nigga was versatile with his shit. You never knew how Remmy was going to do you in.

That was what made him vicious.

"Now," Mane leaned forward as he stared at the row of houses along Patton Street, "the sixth house on the right wit' the white truck parked out front."

"Are you sure?" said Von.

Mane nodded. "That's the house."

In the backseat, Von wrapped the ends of the cord around her hands to get a good grip. Then, she waited until Mane sat back in his seat before looping the cord over his head and around his neck.

Instantly, Remmy sprang forward to prevent Mane from grabbing his gun. He grabbed one arm in a vice grip while patting his body down in search of the weapon he knew Mane kept on his person. The gun was tucked in his waist behind him, and Remmy relieved him of it.

Meanwhile, Mane was struggling under the pressure Von applied against his throat. He reached toward his neck at a futile attempt to stop the cord from biting into his flesh. Von was not having it, as she pressed both of her knees into the back of the passenger seat and pulled back on the ripcord wire with all her might.

"Please!" Mane cried out in desperate fear as the thin wire cut into his throat. Blood spewed, and there was a strangled grunt that came from him.

"Die, nigga! Die," growled Von. Before her, Mane bucked in his seat as he fought for life but was losing the battle. And just like there was nothing going on, Daisy continued driving onward as Mane reached out for her in one last plea for help. All she did was shrug and keep driving.

After another two minutes, Mane was dead. Von slapped him in the back of the head. She hated that he made her go through all that for him to die.

"We dump his ass somewhere and circle back 'round," said Von, trying to catch her breath.

Ten minutes later, they were headed back to Patton Street after dumping Mane out along the street in front of Mount Zion Baptist Church. The truck didn't even stop as Remmy shoved him out the door, and Mane hit the ground rolling.

"Now that that's done," said Von, "we deal wit' this little nigga and take it back home."

"Put us out right here," suggested Remmy. They were about eight houses down from their intended target when the truck stopped, and Von and Remmy got out. They then preceded to walk along the side of the street while the truck proceeded up the street.

As they walked side by side, Von donned her black fitted cap to hide her shoulder length designer braids. She was already outfitted in all-black attire and Soldier Rees.

"Back door or the front?"

Von said, "I got a feelin' that we ain't gon' find him here at the house, Remmy."

"Nothin' beats a failure but a try," said Remmy. "That's what my G-ma used to say."

"We'll see."

Once they made it to the house in question, they both kept their heads low and eased onto its premise like a quiet fog. They surveyed their surroundings as they stealthy made their way around to the back of the house.

Von checked the time on her watch: 2:59 a.m. "We got five minutes to get it done," she whispered.

The house was silent as a dead snitch with his tongue ripped out his mouth. But when Remmy stepped onto the back porch, it creaked, and the sound was loud enough for one to panic. He paused, looked back at Von, and knew what he had to do next. Remmy finally drew his .44 Bulldog, took a deep breath, and charged through the back door with a boom!

Like two vets, they rushed into the house in remarkable formation, one with their back against the other as they moved through the house. It was obvious this was one of the many home invading missions they'd had to do together as a two-man team.

Their movements were precise.

Calculated.

One room after another, they searched from both sides of the hallway but didn't find a living soul.

"I knew it," muttered Von when their mission ended with an unsatisfactory result.

"I don't mind waitin' till he show up."

"Lay on him?" she said.

He nodded. They were standing in the dark living room. Von seemed to be considering the matter at hand. "They gotta come home some time," Remmy said evenly. "He won't even expect it's a trap."

"We can, but that's not gon' happen. It's almost three o'clock in the morning. Avery was bonded outta jail two hours ago. He prolly won't even come home t'night. We'll just be wasting precious time. Nine times outta ten, he's either at the hospital wit' that other little nigga who got sliced up by shorty or he's wit' that other little nigga, Cody. He woulda been home by now if he didn't have either of those two little niggas to own his time."

"So, we look for him at the hospital?" asked Remmy.

"Not before we burn this muthafucker down to the damn ground," said Von.

That made Remmy smile wickedly.

After setting fire to the beds of all three bedrooms and cutting on the gas stove at full blast, Von and Remmy made their exit in a haste. Daisy was right on time pulling up in the truck as they got inside and sped away from the scene.

Where Remmy was expecting to hear the house blow up, it never did come before the SUV distanced itself so far away from the scene that it couldn't be heard.

"You still gonna try that nigga, BJ?" said Daisy, referring to another associate of theirs who lived out in Havana.

"Nah," said Von.

"He might know somethin' useful," insisted Daisy.

"I don't wanna have to kill him too. It's bad enough Mane is dead, and that nigga was one of our best customers. Plus, BJ is too out of the way in Havana to be in the loop of what's going on here in Quincy. Sorry, Dee, you won't be flirting wit' your boytoy t'night, my love." Von didn't mean it to be a joke because she was graveyard serious about this mission.

She was out for blood.

Retaliation.

Chapter 25

Back at the hospital, Shequita checked the time. It was 3:10 a.m., and her body felt like it was trying to shut down on her. Margarette was trying to keep her in focus. Also present in the room was Felicia, Lisa, Tami, and to all of their surprise, Larry "Coach" Thompson, who was Cody and Avery's high school basketball coach and mentor. Somehow, he had found out what was going on and drove to the hospital in the middle of the night to lend what moral support he could offer.

Coach Thompson was horrified as he listened to Tami and Lisa recount what transpired back at the house. To hear of those that died tonight was enough to make the man feel sick to his stomach.

Then, Felicia shared to those who weren't present about what went down between her son and his troubles.

"Where's baby boy now?" asked Lisa.

Felicia shrugged. "He left to go after Ray but never came back," she said.

"Ray Williams? Why was he going after Ray?" Tami perked up at the mention of the last person she expected to be part of the problem.

Silence filled the room.

"What is it?" Tami demanded when she noticed the odd expressions coming from her two closest friends.

Felicia looked away nervously.

"Quita?" Tami rose up to her feet. "What?"

175

"He knows, Tami." That was all she needed to say for Tami to understand what was going on.

"Of course, he ran from the truth like the coward that he is," added Felicia. "So, I sent Av after him, and you know how demanding he can be at times."

"Especially when it comes down to the wellbeing of his brothas," said Shequita.

"I'm lost," Lisa replied all of a sudden.

Tami could damn well imagine how that situation went when Ray was confronted about being Cody's father and what he should be out there doing where his loyalty was concerned.

Tami then turned to Lisa and told her, and Lisa's mouth damn near hit the floor.

"My God," Coach Thompson responded.

"So, Av and him are together right now..." said Felicia but was cut short by the ringing of her phone. She pulled it out of her coat pocket and looked at the screen. "It's Vikki callin' me. I wonder why," she said and answered the phone just as another incoming call came through.

"Felicia? This you, homegirl?"

"What's going on, Vikki?"

"Girl, your house is on fire!" she said frantically.

"What?" Felicia froze.

"It blew the hell up, Felicia. Now, it's just burnin' like crazy right now."

The next thought that came to mind was Avery. *Can he have gone back to the house?* she wondered stressfully. Fear sat on her heart like deadweight. Felicia suddenly could not breathe as thoughts of her son burning and calling out for his mama in the house invaded her mind.

"Felicia, what's wrong?" Shequita and Tami both rushed to her side after seeing the look on her face.

"Av," was the only word that came out of her mouth as she disconnected with Vikki in an attempt to call Ray's phone, only to see that it was Ray who had been calling her from the get-go.

"Is Avery wit' you right now, Felicia?"

"I thought he was wit' you."

Ray said, "No, he was but somethin' happened, and now, I can't find him."

"What happened?"

"Not over the phone, Felicia."

"What happened wit' my fuckin' son, Ray?!" Felicia's eyes were glazed with madness now. Shequita laid a hand upon her sista's shoulder and felt Felicia's body shaking like a wet dog in the middle of a snowstorm.

"Is you still at the hospital right now?"

"Ray!" she screamed outrageously.

"Gimme the phone, sista." Tami snatched the phone away from her and put it to her ear. "What the hell is going on right now, Ray?" she questioned.

"Tami," he said in a frustrated sigh. "Please keep her there wit' you. It's not safe for her to go out there worryin' over Av. I'm on my way. I'll explain everythang when I get there."

"Then you need to get here fast."

"Tami, I promise," he said.

"Get here then, Ray. No exceptions." Tami watched as Felicia pulled away from Shequita and bound for the door.

With the quickness of a cat, Tami ran after her and almost had to tackle her down to the floor at the door.

"Quita, help me!" Tami shouted.

Instead, Lisa sprang into action and ran over to assist her in restraining Felicia.

"Turn me loose! Turn me loose!" Felicia fought against their holds but couldn't get free. Tami was using her strength from the fear of letting Felicia go and losing her forever to some unknown force.

Felicia was bucking like a raging bull and raving in loud bellows of desperate fear and anger. Shequita stepped over to try and talk Felicia out of her wild attitude. It was like talking to a brick wall.

The commotion was so elevated that it sent both Brandi and a female officer to the door. When they looked in and saw three women on one woman, the officer immediately panicked and called for backup.

"That won't be necessary," Margarette yelled over the ruckus they were causing.

Right then, Marolyn entered the room after being interrogated for the second time in regard to her husband's actions. When she saw what was happening, she gazed over at Margarette for an explanation.

"Let's just break it up," Margarette suggested.

And that was exactly what they did. Together, both women joined in to break up the commotion. By this time, two more police officers showed up, and Felicia was too exhausted to even care to continue.

When questioned by the more superior officer, it was Coach who assured them that all was well, that Felicia had just received some terrible news, and her reaction was cause to be regulated by her sistas.

"Y'all are just too much in this room," said the female officer with the shake of her big head.

"Bitch, kick rocks!" Shequita said to her back as she was leaving out the room.

"Now can somebody please tell me what that was really all about just now?" said Marolyn.

"What did Vikki say to you?" Lisa asked Felicia once she had finally taken a seat beside Teddy's bed. She even looked exhausted, her hair all wild and her big, juicy, pink lips ashen-dry.

Felicia licked her lips and told them what Vikki had related to her.

"Damn," Brandi had to take a seat next. This was just too damn much for her to take in one night. It was like the drama and pain was never going to end.

"And that's why Ray said to keep her here, y'all. That it's not safe for her to be going out there," Tami exclaimed.

"I agree," said Shequita.

"But what if Av's gone to the house? What if my baby is in there?" Felicia cried sorrowfully. In all the years her sistas had known her, they'd never seen her this shaken up in her life.

No one could reassure her of her fears because they did not know the actual truth.

Avery could very well be in that house.

Or he wasn't.

It was a hard pill to swallow.

~   ~   ~

Lounging across the backseat of Kelli's navy-blue Ford Explorer with its dark tinted windows, Avery groaned in pure agony. Every pothole in the road or too sharp of a turn, it created an unnerving pain shooting through his body like a lightning bolt.

"Sorry, Av!" Kelli would say when she sensed that her bumpy driving had caused him discomfort.

So far, they had driven through the Lake Skillet neighborhood and were damn near pulled over by the police. Through a neighboring source of Rayneshia's, it was told that another shooting had transpired, and a cop was killed.

Then, they were on to the Sub-Division area where another patrol unit was lurking, and no one was in sight — no dopeheads, no drunks, hustlas, nobody was roaming the streets. That was a first being that Sub-D was always alive with nonstop activities going on even in the wee hours of the night like right now.

The whole hood seemed dead.

And that was worrisome.

Shooting over across to Pepper Hill, you could see the sky overhead glowing in the dark from emergency lights flashing about, including the large ball of fire, which was Avery's house, but they hadn't made it that far yet where he could see it. But when he did, it was going to change him in a way like never before.

That was when they saw little Bebop jetting past the front of the truck's headlights on his speed bike. Kelli had to stomp on the brakes fast in order not to run him over.

"Bebop! Stop him, Kay-Kay!" Avery replied.

"How the hell am I gonna do that?!" she shot back at him as she looked to her left. Bebop was pedaling frantically and quickly distancing himself from them. The boy was flying down the street.

"Follow him," said Avery.

"Follow him?"

"Just do it, Kay-Kay!"

Kelli whipped the wheel sharply, and in the process, she had to bounce over a curb to the right of the vehicle along the street in pursuit of Bebop.

Despite his discomfort, Avery had to smile at Bebop's way of handling the bike. Ever since Teddy had given him that bike, fast and faster were the only speeds he knew, like a rocket. Usually, there was no catching him while on his bike, but the truck caught up with him in no time.

"Bebop?!" Avery had wound down his side window as the truck suddenly came up alongside of Bebop and his speed bike.

When the boy recognized his voice and saw his face, Bebop slammed on brakes with a nice hook-slide halt that he'd mastered over time.

"Av," Bebop jumped off the bike and rushed over to the rear passenger door, "where you been?" he said breathlessly. "I just came from your house. It's on fire! Somethin' exploded in it, heard it way 'cross the neighborhood. Alisha is dead. Wes…"

"Wait, wait, wait!" Avery cut him off. "Did you say my house is on fire?" he panicked.

Bebop gave him a strange look. Then, he reached to open the door and told Avery to move over.

From behind the wheel, Kelli watched the exchange between Bebop and Avery and knew some type of bond was shared between the two.

"What about your bike?" asked Rayneshia.

"Oh, shit!" Bebop muttered, thought about it, then he said, "Nobody ain't gon' steal my bike. Everybody knows that's my bike." Then, he was impressed when Rayneshia got out and took up his bike and deposited it into the back cabin of the truck. He turned to Avery and said, "Is she your girlfriend?"

"Bebop." Avery gave him that stern tone of voice.

Rayneshia blushed in the dark.

Almost in a scared, excited way of expression, Bebop told his big brotha all that had been going on.

At the same time, Kelli made her way in the direction of Avery's house. They could hear the fire truck blaring in the night as it neared.

Avery was so devastated over what Bebop had shared with him of the tragedies of the night. Alisha. Wesley. Corey. They all were dead, gunned down by a drive-by shooter, one that Avery knew was now living on borrowed time — if they hadn't already been sought after and slain by Cody and his murderous crew that he had with him.

"Cody told me to watch over Mama Tee and protect her, but she upped and left me," said Bebop. "And now I don't know where she at, Av."

Avery draped an arm around the boy's bony shoulders.

"Cody gon' be mad at me now," said Bebop.

"No, he won't," Avery assured him. Then, they turned onto Patton Street where the whole area was aglow from the great fireball that was his home.

"Ohmigod," Rayneshia gasped.

Kelli cried, "I'm so sorry, Avery." She brought the truck to a stop along the side of the street.

"Help me out the truck, Bebop."

"You hurt, big brotha?" He gazed up at Avery.

"Just help me, lil brah," said Avery in a strained voice that made Bebop worry that he was about to cry for what was happening to his house.

Without further ado, Bebop jumped out of the truck and hurried around to the other side at once. He helped Avery down from the truck, and together, they approached the burning furnace of his childhood home.

Also present along the street was at least ten to fifteen people standing off from the big, blazing fire across the street. All it took was for one person to see him, and all eyes turned in his direction.

But nobody really didn't have anything to say for fear of saying the wrong thing.

"Stay right here, Bebop," Avery told the boy as he uncurled his arm from around his neck to take a closer look at the burning house.

"Av?" It was Vikki that came out of nowhere to rush over to him. She was a big woman, top heavy, and her approach was full of action.

"Who did this shit, Vikki?" he asked.

"I don't know, baby."

"You live next door to our house, Vikki. You gotta have seen somethin'," he argued evenly.

"Only a truck," Vikki said after a long thought.

"A truck? What kinda truck?"

She described the SUV to him. "It circled around a few times but..." Vikki was interrupted by the loud roar of the fire truck turning onto the street up ahead. When she turned back to face Avery, he was already headed back toward the truck.

Standing outside the truck was Rayneshia, who Bebop was standing next to, looking just as disturbed as he knew Avery felt at that moment.

Avery climbed into the back of the truck without any assistance.

Bebop got in beside him. "I hate this shit."

No one said a word.

They hated it too.

And then he cried. It was not because of what had been done but because of what he was going to do to the person that did it.

Because there would be no turning back.

Because they had hurt his family.

Chapter 26

When Money Mel got the call about the house fire and informed Cody on the issue, Cody remained silent while worrying whether someone was in the house or not.

"No one knows if anybody was inside or not," said Money Mel, who received the call from Samantha Harris, who actually lived directly across the street from Avery's house. "But she did say she saw Av out there t'night," he added.

That brought Cody's head upright. "Out where? I thought Av's in the Tent?" he replied.

"Me too," said Money Mel.

Could this be true? Or could Samantha have mistaken his brotha for someone else? Cody wasn't sure how he should take this but knew he needed further confirmation on the matter. He asked Twan if he could use his phone, and it was given to him without hesitation.

Cody called Felicia. If anybody knew anything regarding Avery, it would definitely be her.

The phone was answered on the second ring. But it wasn't his brotha's mother that answered. "Who is this?" Cody demanded.

"Is this Av?" came a female's voice.

He paused. "No. Av's my brotha. This Cody. Lemme speak to Felicia," he replied.

"She's not here right now, Cody."

"Who is this?"

184

Before she could answer, Cody heard his own mother's voice in the background demanding the phone. At the sound of his mother's voice, Cody thought back on their last encounter back at the house. It was her blessing why he was back out in the field on that gangsta shit.

Mama said go handle that, so who was he not to honor her wishes?

"Baby? What's going on?" Tami came over the other end of the phone.

"Ma, is Av out right now?"

Pause.

"Yeah. He made it out earlier. Are you okay, baby? I wanna see you."

"Where is Av? How did he get out?" Cody didn't want to believe it, but he knew Avery was one daring guy, and at first opportunity, he would have escaped from the juvenile detention center if he could.

His mother gave him the lowdown on Avery's situation, and Cody wasn't surprised to hear what he was being told.

"So, that's the last time you saw my brotha?"

"Yep," she said.

"But why is he wit' Mr. Ray?"

Another pause.

"It's a long story, baby, but you'll know well enough about it later."

Cody skipped over that response. "I need to see my brotha, Ma. Can you call Mr. Ray and see what's up? Have them meet us somewhere?" he asked.

"You still wit' Melvin?"

"Yeah," he answered. "He's right here."

Tami said, "Baby, as soon as I can reach him, I'll make sure that he contacts you because we believe he's prolly out there lookin' for you as well."

Those words gave him hope. "Did you hear about the fire at his house?"

"We heard."

"So, where is Ms. Felicia?" Cody hoped like hell she didn't tell him that Felicia had left for her house. He didn't want to torture himself with the thought of her having been in the house when it caught afire.

"She's safe. Felicia just stepped out for a minute. She's wit' Quita, baby. She knows, and it's really hard on her right now, Cody."

"I know," Cody murmured softly.

Next to him, Souljah's phone rang, and he answered it immediately, greeting the caller in his Kutthroat Kommittee gang jargon that hailed from his roots in Jacksonville, Florida. Souljah, better known as Skeet in his hometown of Duval County, was a westside representative and a real deal young beast mode type of nigga.

Cody spoke with his mother for a few more moments, reminding her that his contact with Avery was vital and that she needed to make it happen.

"I love you, baby," Tami told her son.

Cody hesitated. "Love you too, Ma. Find Av," he said and hung up the phone. Then, he sat back in his seat and let out a deep breath, his chest still hurting from when the bullet had struck him.

They were back in Pepper Hill as Money Mel thought it would be good to stop by his own childhood home to check up on things there.

"There's suspicion that the house exploded before it burned down," said Twan, staring down at the screen of his cell phone after Cody gave it back to him.

"Exploded?"

"Yeah. People said they heard it blow up first, then it was on fire. I think that was done deliberately. Because I don't believe in coincidences, my nigga. That was a hit and..." Twan was interrupted by Cody.

"Who would be targetin' Av?" he replied.

"Didn't Mama Tee say brah was wit' Mr. Ray? He's a homicide detective. What the fuck is he doing wit' him?" Money Mel interjected.

"I don't know." Cody told him what his mother said. "She acts like it's some big secret or somethin', but somethin' tells me whatever it is she didn't wanna talk about it over the phone."

"Prolly because two people just got slumped outside his crib," said Souljah.

"Huh?" This shocked Twan. "What?"

Money Mel brought the car to a halt at the curb in front of his mother's house. Her old Toyota Corolla was parked in the driveway, which meant that she had taken the Dodge Magnum out tonight instead.

When Cody asked Souljah to explain what he meant, he did so with pleasure.

The call had come from his side chick, Whitney, who actually lived on Lee Road, which was not that for from the detective's house. She was still on the scene watching the procession as the CSI team and cops and other potential officials secured the crime scene.

"There's word that the shootout was between the two dead niggas and another young nigga," said Souljah.

"Av?" said Cody.

"Whoever he is, the detective dude is hidin' him out in his crib. At least that's what Whitney believes, but she did say another person got away though."

Right then, Money Mel's phone rang, and he answered it after not recognizing the number.

"Hello?"

"Mel!" It was Avery. "Brah, where you at? Is Cody wit' you?!" came a breathless reply.

In the quietness of the car, Cody's ears perked up at the unmistakable sound of his brotha's voice. Then, he reached between the two front seats and took the phone away from Money Mel before he could say anything further to Avery.

"I'm right here, Av," he said.

"Cody?"

"What up, brah? Where you at, Av?"

"Where are you?"

"I'm at Teddy's house," Cody told him as he felt a burning sigh of relief spreading in his chest.

"Stay right there," Avery replied before saying something to someone else, then he said to Cody, "I'm on my way there right now, Cody. You okay?"

"I am now," Cody said.

And those words were music to his own ears because now Cody was sure that his brotha was indeed alright. But little did he know the trouble that was out there lurking and determined to destroy everything he ever loved.

~   ~   ~

The squeaking of car brakes was heard pulling up outside Meesha's house as she sat on the front sofa in her living room nursing a cup of Seagram's gin and apple juice.

She rose up to her corn-toed, bare feet and stepped over to the window. Her arms and lower back were still sore after removing the bloody sofa outside, to the back, and scrubbing the floors and other areas where Menace's blood had touched. It was a very strenuous task, but she accomplished it faithfully.

Just when she was relaxing with a nice drink, there came someone else pulling up outside her house. Meesha looked and saw that it was Lamar's car, and then she started to really panic.

This was what she was hoping to not happen. And she had a strange feeling why he decided to want to show up now that all this was going on.

That dumb bitch, Renee Lane. The sneaky bitch who lived two houses over and was fuckin' her man on the low.

Renee was evil-minded and would do whatever she could to tarnish her name.

And Lamar's stupid ass always seemed to take her word for it — and the other peoples' word where her business with other niggas was concerned.

They were no longer together now, hadn't been for about six years now, but her and Lamar did share a son together. LJ was seven years old now, and as for her five-year- old, Royaltee Monique Bunion, that was what struck a nerve in Lamar when he found out that her beautiful little girl wasn't his. Lamar punched her in her face and body slammed her ass to the floor and threatened to kill her for crossing him the way she did.

But it was okay for him to mess around with other bitches behind her back. When she gave him a taste of his own medicine, he couldn't handle the outcome.

Royaltee was an unexpected blessing with her second baby daddy, Rhalo, but unfortunately for him, he was in prison for shooting Lamar three times. All he had to hear was that Lamar had assaulted her while she was pregnant with his daughter, and Rhalotried to kill him for that.

Meatball was a standup guy.

He was respectable.

A real gangsta.

Now, there Lamar was at her door, knocking loudly like he didn't have any sense. Twice Meesha had to change the locks on her door after the nigga somehow managed to possess a key to her home. She made her way over to the front door and opened it for him.

"What you got going on in here, Meesha?" Lamar was of a tall, slender physique, brown skin tone, gold teeth, and a shiny, bald head. He brushed past her into the house.

"What you mean what I got going on, Lamar? It's damn near four somethin' in the morning." She shut the door and turned to face him.

Lamar gave her a dumb look.

"Like that stops you from doing anythang." He shrugged and sensed the smell of bleach and Pine Sol in the air.

"What do you want, Lamar?"

"Where's my son?"

Meesha shot him an are-you-serious expression. "LJ is in his room asleep," she answered grudgingly.

"What happened to the couch?" Lamar was looking around the living room suspiciously and had noticed that the larger sofa was missing.

"Nigga, what the fuck do you want?" she snapped.

"Who else is here wit' you and my son?" The question made Meesha want to punch his ass in the face, only because he left out the fact that Royaltee was part of the equation. Ever since he found out she wasn't his, it was Lamar's way of tormenting Meesha to mistreat her daughter and make her feel unloved.

How did Lamar know that someone else besides her children was in the house?

That bitch, Renee.

Before it was all said and done, Meesha was going to tear Renee a new asshole. The heifer just didn't know how to stay the fuck out of her business.

Because Meesha had taken too long to answer his question, Lamar headed down the hallway to see for himself. Instant fear enveloped Meesha as she hurried along after him, knowing Lamar would discover the other man occupying the spare bedroom.

And that was exactly where he directed his focus as if he already knew what he would find there.

Meesha was going to kill Renee Lane.

"Lamar, no!" said Meesha when he reached for the door handle of the guest room.

Lamar ignored her and opened the door. He stepped inside the room, but that one step was all he took before he was stepping back out with his hands up in a surrendering fashion.

A minute later, Meesha watched as Menace, his good arm extended before him as he clutched a Glock .40, stepped forward into the hallway. The gun was aimed directly at Lamar's face.

"This what you lookin' for, nigga?" Menace's face was grim, his words slurred a little from the heavy dose of medication, and his bandaged arm in a makeshift sling going across his chest. His larger bandage wound covering was wrapped around his stomach area, and it was blotched with the slow leak of blood.

This scared the shit out of Meesha, but it also felt damn good to see Lamar bitch up to the man with the gun in his face.

"It's all good, homeboy," said Lamar. "I didn't know this was what it was about."

"What is it about?"

"You hurt," Lamar pointed out.

Menace shook his head slowly. "Nah, nigga. I ain't hurt. I'm reenergized," he said.

Chapter 27

Fifteen minutes after Mane's body was discovered in the street, the SUV that Von was riding in was pulling up into the entrance of the local hospital.

The last of the few stragglers that the fire alarm emergency had encouraged their immediate exit was now reentering the building. The truck slowly made its way through the vehicle packed parking lot area and had to circle around once before it located a vacant space.

This position provided a view of the front and the side entrances of the building. It was a small hospital compared to Tallahassee Memorial Hospital, which was gigantic in size with its own parking garage above the structure and on its grounds.

To Von, it shouldn't be all that difficult to find who she was looking for. The hospital was small enough where she was liable to walk right inside and probably bump into her man.

"I can go in there and scope thangs out and maybe get some information on what we need to capitalize from," said Daisy.

"Not by yourself," said Von.

Daisy said, "To go solo is the best way, Von. You can't go because you got blood on your clothes, and your face is well known. Need I to remind you of your last visit down here in Quincy when a bitch got shot in both of her legs?"

Von looked up at her in quiet earnest.

"And not you either, Remmy. It's too much going on in this crazy town for a muthafucker to suspect you, a stranger, and begin askin' questions. Just your presence alone oozes 'killa', and we don't need you to be on the scene unless the circumstances warrants it." Daisy sounded as though she was enjoying this part.

"And what makes you so special?" Remmy replied.

"First of all, I'm a woman," said Daisy. "And my presence is less threatening, and besides, I can talk a cat off a fish tank," she boasted.

"More like the teeth outta a shark," muttered Remmy.

Daisy beamed and thanked him for the compliment then opened the door and got out. As she made her way for the front door, it opened, and two older women stepped out. One of them pulled out a cigarette and put flame to it. At the same time, another car pulled up on the scene, and both women reacted toward its presence as if they were anticipating whoever it was occupying the approaching car.

"There goes Ray right there," said Shequita, not paying Daisy too much attention now that the car captured her focus.

Daisy had just walked past them for the door when the next thing she heard gave her pause.

"But I don't see Avery in the car wit' him," said Felicia, taking another pull from her cigarette.

Avery? thought Daisy for a brief second, then she let herself into the building without a backwards glance. She had to maintain her game face and not let what she'd just heard alter her current mission.

Back in the truck, Von and Remmy were both observing the approaching vehicle as it drove up and parked next to the Emergency Room entrance section of the building.

"Oh, shit!" Von cussed.

"What? Oh, shit what?" said Remmy.

Before she answered, Von thought about how right Daisy was about her showing her face.

"That's that homicide detective nigga I had bumped heads wit' a couple times when my niggas, Bear and Peanut, got killed outside the Platinum Club a few years ago, and I shut the bitch down. Then, about two months ago when I saw the nigga in Havana at a gas station, the pussy nigga remembered me from that Platinum Club shit and called himself tryna intimidate me like I'm some chump."

"What he do?"

Von watched the detective exit his car and approach the two women standing out front.

"He claimed he was watchin' me and that if I'm not careful, he gon' make me his bitch."

"He said that?" said Remmy, amused.

"Yeah."

"And what did you say? I know you said some slick shit back at him."

Von remembered that moment like it was yesterday. "I told him that I'm already his bitch," she said. "The wrong bitch that's gon' break his heart if he so much as violate my personal space again."

"Then it was wise that you do stay in the truck," he explained to Von. "We don't need you bumpin' heads wit' him again t'night."

"I'll kill that muthafucker!"

"I know you would, my nigga. But let's not hope that he gives you a reason to do it tonight."

Just looking at the detective made Von want to put a bullet through his brain. The man had really rubbed her the wrong way, and it still irked her that she hadn't made him suffer for it.

In front of the building, it looked like a heated confrontation was being held between the detective and the two women. The one smoking the cigarette drew back a clenched fist to punch him but was gently restrained by the other woman.

"Shoulda punched his bitch ass," said Remmy.

Von couldn't have agreed more.

It was another fourteen minutes later when Daisy made her exit from the building. Ray and the others had gone inside by this time and weren't expected to come back out anytime soon.

The way Daisy was hurrying back toward the truck and looking back over her shoulder made her appear as though she was running from something.

"What'chu got?" Von replied the instant Daisy slid back in behind the wheel.

"We might have just struck gold," she said. Then, Daisy shared with them what all she knew. She had found the remedy that would end it all tonight.

~   ~   ~

The gang was in the living room, chillin' and talking amongst each other, when Twan exited from the kitchen where he'd conducted a very important phone conversation with one of his top sources.

Cody was lounging in Teddy's favorite beanbag chair beside Souljah, who was conversing with Money Mel about purchasing some new artillery.

"Mane is dead," said Twan.

Everybody looked up at him in astonishment. It was no question that they all knew who Mane was.

"That was a source of mines that works for the QPD — that doesn't leave this room. Anyway, Mane was found dead in Pepper Hill not too far from here. But his car was found at Twenty-Four, which means whoever killed him dumped him here in the hood," Twan said and perched on the arm of the sofa chair beside Souljah.

"Wonder who killed him," said Money Mel.

"I think my source is about to review the camera footage outside the gas station to see what they can learn from there."

"That should narrow it down," said Souljah. "Whoever he left Twenty-Four wit' will show on video."

A text message came through Money Mel's phone from Avery to inform that he was pulling up outside. When he delivered the message, Cody jumped up and groaned in agony but still managed to go to the front door. He couldn't wait to see his brotha.

A pair of headlights approached from the street until a familiar Ford Explorer came fully into view and parked behind the Mercury.

"Cody!" Bebop was the first person to get out the SUV and then hurry around to the other side to help Avery.

When Cody saw this, he rushed to his brotha's aid at once.

"I'm good," Avery smirked painfully at him.

"What happened?" Cody wasn't trying to hear that 'I'm good' bullshit and still reached out to assist Avery and keep him balanced.

"He got jumped," said Bebop.

Cody paused. "Jumped? By who?"

Avery only said that he wanted to go inside, and Cody nodded solemnly. Together, Bebop and Cody escorted Avery toward the front door while Rayneshia and Kelli followed quietly behind.

A police cruiser slowly drove by along the street but didn't bother stopping to investigate. It just kept right on rollin', and they all entered the house without incident.

Once they were all settled around the living room with Cody sharing the big beanbag chair with Avery, he looked worriedly over at his brotha.

"What happened to you, brah?" asked Cody.

Avery sighed and told him everything.

As he listened, Cody thought back on how he handled things back at the Pit. What Avery was describing at the moment was a traumatic experience. His survival instincts caused him to black out and kill two people. The fact that his brotha had to go through that reawakened Cody's inner beast.

He wished he could resurrect Trent and his homeboy and kill them both all over again.

"Then that explains who the two bodies belong to," said Souljah. "Any idea who the third person was?"

Avery shook his head no.

"He can be anybody," said Money Mel.

Right then, Cody stood up, and then, he helped Avery up to his feet. He wanted to speak with him privately and led the way back to Teddy's room.

Bebop got up to follow, but Money Mel told him to sit his ass down.

Rayneshia pulled the boy down protectively next to her, and Bebop was all for it.

Shutting the bedroom door to keep the others out, Cody watched as Avery struggled over to Teddy's unmade bed and sat down. He then grabbed the spot where he was hurting the most, and Cody was suddenly overwhelmed with sadness, seeing him like this.

It hurt him to see Avery like this.

"I killed somebody tonight too," said Cody.

Avery lifted his gaze up at him.

"I lost it, brah."

Then, he shared with Avery his greatest fear.

Silent tears spilled from Avery's eyes as he heard and understood his brotha's pain.

Cody then dropped down on the bed next to him. There was no words that heeded further speaking. Together, they shared the same fears and pain, as they leaned on one another for strength.

Footsteps were heard hurrying down the hall toward the bedroom, and a second later, Rayneshia was heard calling after Avery from the other side.

"Get that for me, brah. Let her in," said Avery.

As he remained sitting on the bed, Avery kicked himself mentally for not telling Cody the truth about Ray. He knew it would crush his brotha, and hurting Cody further was the last thing he wanted to do.

The door opened, and Rayneshia flurried through the door inside the room, carrying what Avery recognized as Shequita's tablet computer in her possession.

"Is this one of the ones you went through it wit' tonight, Av?" said Rayneshia, turning the face of the tablet screen around, so he could see.

Avery instantly recognized the two faces of the guys that accompanied Trent tonight. There were a total of five people in all in the Instagram photo, but Avery would never forget those faces as long as he lived, especially the one he had killed next to Trent in the photo then the bigger one of them all standing in the background.

"Yeah," he answered.

"Point 'em out to me."

When Avery pointed them out and singled out the one he said had gotten away, Rayneshia went about swiping and tapping the tablet screen as she busied herself doing whatever it was she was doing.

"I figured lookin' into Trent's available links would tell us just who those other two guys might be. And now that I got their identities, I am running them through my daddy's coded CCI database to get us a name or whatever it is we can use to locate the one that got away. And so far his name appears to be Tyler Mckenzie," she said.

"Tyler Mckenzie?" Cody thought the name sounded a little familiar but couldn't quite connect it.

"He's from Tallahassee. Went to Godby High School, dropped out in the ninth grade. He was born twenty-two years ago. His gang affiliation is Folk Nation, the Seven-Four GDs. Criminal history: breakin' and enterin', battery, petty theft, and a list of violent charges." Rayneshia paused momentarily to let that sink in as she regarded both of them closely.

"Does Tyler have hobbies? An address? Where in Tallahassee he can be found?" asked Avery.

"I can assure you that it's all there."

"Why are you doing this, Rayneshia? Aren't you scared this shit could hurt you too? I mean, look how close this shit has come to jeopardizin' your life tonight," said Cody.

Avery remained quiet.

"Why do you even care whether I care or not, Cody? As long as you can seek revenge of those who crossed you and your family is all that matters, right?" Rayneshia was now standing face to face with Cody, her deep brown eyes intense and piercing.

"I just don't want nobody else to get hurt."

"But is it vengeance you want?"

Slowly, Cody nodded his head.

"Why?" he replied. "What's wit' all the questions?"

She looked him dead in the eyes. "Because you are my brotha, Cody, and I want nothing more than to help you accomplish your mission."

"You don't even know me," Cody told her.

"And you're right, Cody." Rayneshia stood firm before him, and Avery suddenly held his breath. "But that still doesn't change the fact that we share the same bloodline."

He froze. "The same bloodline?"

"We are siblings, Cody."

"The fuck are you talkin' about?" Cody retorted.

And so, Rayneshia told him the truth.

The bomb dropped.

And then, all hell broke loose.

To Be Continued…

Lock Down Publications and Ca$h Presents
Assisted Publishing Packages

Due to an increase in the price of services we have increased our prices. The prices below reflect the price increase as of 11/1/24.

BASIC PACKAGE **$699** Editing Cover Design Formatting	UPGRADED PACKAGE **$1000** Typing Editing Cover Design Formatting Upload eBooks to Amazon Upload Paperback to Amazon
ADVANCE PACKAGE **$1,400** Typing Editing (line editing/content) Cover Design Formatting Copyright Registration Proofreading Upload eBooks to Amazon Upload Paperback to Amazon	**LDP SUPREME PACKAGE** **$1,700** Typing Editing (line editing/content) Cover Design Formatting Copyright Registration Proofreading Set up Amazon Account Upload eBooks to Amazon Upload Paperback to Amazon Advertise on LDP's Amazon and Facebook Page

***Other services available upon request.
Additional charges may apply

Lock Down Publications
P.O. Box 944
Stockbridge, GA 30281-9998
Phone: 470 303-9761
Email: lockdownpublications@gmail.com

Submission Guideline

Submit the first three chapters of your completed manuscript to ldpsubmissions@gmail.com. In the subject line add **Your Book's Title**. The manuscript must be in a Word Doc file and sent as an attachment. Document should be in Times New Roman, double spaced, and in size 12 font. Also, provide your synopsis and full contact information. If sending multiple submissions, they must each be in a separate email.

Have a story but no way to send it electronically? You can still submit to LDP/Ca$h Presents. Send in the first three chapters, written or typed, of your completed manuscript to:

LDP: Submissions Dept
P.O. Box 944
Stockbridge, GA 30281-9998

DO NOT send original manuscript. Must be a duplicate. Provide your synopsis and a cover letter containing your full contact information.

Thanks for considering LDP and Ca$h Presents.

NEW RELEASES

BLOODLINE OF A SAVAGE 1,2&3
THESE VICIOUS STREETS 1,2&3
RELENTLESS GOON
RELENTLESS GOON 2
BY PRINCE A. TAUHID

THE BUTTERFLY MAFIA 1-3
BY FUMIYA PAYNE

A THUG'S STREET PRINCESS 1,2&3
BY MEESHA

CITY OF SMOKE 1& 2
BY MOLOTTI

STEPPERS 1,2&3
THE REAL BADDIES OF CHI-RAQ
BY KING RIO

THE LANE 1&2
BY KEN-KEN SPENCE

THUG OF SPADES 1,2&3
LOVE IN THE TRENCHES 2
CORNER BOY CHRONICLES
BY COREY ROBINSON

TIL DEATH 3
BY ARYANNA

THE BIRTH OF A GANGSTER 4
BY DELMONT PLAYER

FRESH OFF DA PORCH | IRA B.

PRODUCT OF THE STREETS 1&2
BY DEMOND "MONEY" ANDERSON

NO TIME FOR ERROR
BY KEESE

MONEY HUNGRY DEMONS 1,2&3
BY TRANAY ADAMS

HUNGRY FOR MONEY 1&2
BY SLIMBOS

A THUGGISH PASSION
KILLAZ ON STANDBY 1&2
LAND OF DA HOOLIGANZ 1,2&3
FRESH OFF DA PORCH
BY IRA B.

COUNTDOWN OF A KILLA 1&2
GUNS DOWN, BOTTOMS UP 1&2
SEX, MURDA AND GOD
BY LO-LIFE

THE LEVEL UP 1&2
BY LUXURY KING

FO'EVA ROLLIN' 1&2
BY ASSA RAYMOND BAKER

HUB CITY MENACE 1&2
BY J. WHITE

KILLA CREW
DYING FOR LIKES
BY ARYANNA

FRESH OFF DA PORCH | IRA B.

IF YOU CROSS ME ONCE 6
ANGEL 5
By Anthony Fields

IMMA DIE BOUT MINE 5
By Aryanna

A THUGS STREET PRINCESS 3
EMBRACING THE LOVE OF A BOSS
By Meesha

PRODUCT OF THE STREETS 3
By Demond Money Anderson

STANDING ON HER BUSINESS
BY DG SANTANA

GET IT IN SLUGS 1&2
B. STALLS

CORNER BOYS 2
By Corey Robinson

THE MURDER QUEENS 6&7
By Michael Gallon

CITY OF SMOKE 3
By Molotti

CONFESSIONS OF A DOPEBOY
By Nicholas Lock

TENDER
BY KHUFU

THA TAKEOVER
By Keith Chandler

BETRAYAL OF A G 2
By Ray Vinci

CRIME BOSS 4
By Playa Ray

Coming Soon from Lock Down Publications/Ca$h Presents

RAN OFF ON THE PLUG 2 by **PAPER BOI RARI**
STREET REDEMPTION by **TONY DANIELS**
SAVAGE FAMILY EMPIRE by **PRINCE TAUHID**
BAD BITCHES WIT' GUNZ by **DIESEL**
THE SINGLE LADIES by **DIESEL**
COKE BY THE TRUCKLOAD by **DIESEL**
PROBLEM SOLVED by **DIESEL**
TIPPIN' THE SCALES by **DIESEL**
OPPS CRY TOO by **SAYNOMORE**
A GANGSTA'S KARMA by **FLAME**

AVAILABLE NOW

RESTRAINING ORDER 1 & 2
By **CA$H & Coffee**

LOVE KNOWS NO BOUNDARIES 1-3
By **Coffee**

RAISED AS A GOON I, II, III & IV
BRED BY THE SLUMS I, II, III
BLAST FOR ME I & II
ROTTEN TO THE CORE I II III
A BRONX TALE I, II, III
DUFFLE BAG CARTEL I II III IV V VI
HEARTLESS GOON I II III IV V
A SAVAGE DOPEBOY I II
DRUG LORDS I II III
CUTTHROAT MAFIA I II
KING OF THE TRENCHES
By **Ghost**

LAY IT DOWN I & II
LAST OF A DYING BREED I II
BLOOD STAINS OF A SHOTTA I & II III
By **Jamaica**

LOYAL TO THE GAME I II III
LIFE OF SIN I, II III
By **TJ & Jelissa**

IF LOVING HIM IS WRONG…I & II
LOVE ME EVEN WHEN IT HURTS I II III
By **Jelissa**

PUSH IT TO THE LIMIT
By **Bre' Hayes**

BLOODY COMMAS I & II
SKI MASK CARTEL I, II & III
KING OF NEW YORK I II, III IV V
RISE TO POWER I II III
COKE KINGS I II III IV V
BORN HEARTLESS I II III IV
KING OF THE TRAP I II
By **T.J. Edwards**

WHEN THE STREETS CLAP BACK I & II III
THE HEART OF A SAVAGE I II III IV
MONEY MAFIA I II
LOYAL TO THE SOIL I II III
By **Jibril Williams**

A DISTINGUISHED THUG STOLE MY HEART I - III
LOVE SHOULDN'T HURT I II III IV
RENEGADE BOYS 1-4
PAID IN KARMA 1-3
SAVAGE STORMS 1-3
AN UNFORESEEN LOVE 1-3
BABY, I'M WINTERTIME COLD 1-3
A THUG'S STREET PRINCESS 1&2
By **Meesha**

CUM FOR ME 1-8
An LDP Erotica Collaboration

BLOOD OF A BOSS 1-5
SHADOWS OF THE GAME
TRAP BASTARD
By **Askari**

A GANGSTER'S CODE 1-3
A GANGSTER'S SYN 1-3
THE SAVAGE LIFE 1-3
CHAINED TO THE STREETS 1-3
BLOOD ON THE MONEY 1-3
A GANGSTA'S PAIN 1-3
BEAUTIFUL LIES AND UGLY TRUTHS
CHURCH IN THESE STREETS
By **J-Blunt**

THE STREETS BLEED MURDER 1-3
THE HEART OF A GANGSTA 1-3
By **Jerry Jackson**

WHEN A GOOD GIRL GOES BAD
By **Adrienne**

THE COST OF LOYALTY 1-3
By **Kweli**

BRIDE OF A HUSTLA 1-3
THE FETTI GIRLS 1-3
CORRUPTED BY A GANGSTA 1-4
BLINDED BY HIS LOVE
THE PRICE YOU PAY FOR LOVE 1-3
DOPE GIRL MAGIC 1-3
By **Destiny Skai**

A KINGPIN'S AMBITION
A KINGPIN'S AMBITION II
I MURDER FOR THE DOUGH
By **Ambitious**

A DOPEBOY'S PRAYER
By **Eddie "Wolf" Lee**

TRUE SAVAGE 1-7
DOPE BOY MAGIC 1-3
MIDNIGHT CARTEL 1-3
CITY OF KINGZ 1&2
NIGHTMARE ON SILENT AVE
THE PLUG OF LIL MEXICO 1&2
CLASSIC CITY
By **Chris Green**

LOVE & CHASIN' PAPER
By **Qay Crockett**

THE KING CARTEL 1-3
By **Frank Gresham**

THESE NIGGAS AIN'T LOYAL 1-3
By **Nikki Tee**

GANGSTA SHYT 1-3
By **CATO**

THE ULTIMATE BETRAYAL
By **Phoenix**

BOSS'N UP 1-3
By **Royal Nicole**

I LOVE YOU TO DEATH
By **Destiny J**

BROOKLYN HUSTLAZ
By **Boogsy Morina**

GANGSTA CITY
By **Teddy Duke**

TO DIE IN VAIN
SINS OF A HUSTLA
By **ASAD**

I RIDE FOR MY HITTA
I STILL RIDE FOR MY HITTA
By **Misty Holt**

A GANGSTER'S REVENGE 1-4
THE BOSS MAN'S DAUGHTERS 1-5
A SAVAGE LOVE 1&2
BAE BELONGS TO ME 1&2
A HUSTLER'S DECEIT 1-3
WHAT BAD BITCHES DO 1-3
SOUL OF A MONSTER 1-3
KILL ZONE
A DOPE BOY'S QUEEN 1-3
TIL DEATH 1-3
IMMA DIE BOUT MINE 1-5
By **Aryanna**

BROOKLYN ON LOCK 1 & 2
By **Sonovia**

A DRUG KING AND HIS DIAMOND 1-3
A DOPEMAN'S RICHES
HER MAN, MINE'S TOO 1&2
CASH MONEY HO'S
THE WIFEY I USED TO BE 1&2
PRETTY GIRLS DO NASTY THINGS
By **Nicole Goosby**

THE STREETS ARE CALLING
By **Duquie Wilson**

FRESH OFF DA PORCH | IRA B.

LIPSTICK KILLAH 1-3
CRIME OF PASSION 1-3
FRIEND OR FOE 1-3
By **Mimi**

TRAPHOUSE KING 1-3
KINGPIN KILLAZ 1-3
STREET KINGS 1&2
PAID IN BLOOD 1&2
CARTEL KILLAZ 1-3
DOPE GODS 1&2
By **Hood Rich**

STEADY MOBBN' 1-3
THE STREETS STAINED MY SOUL 1-3
By **Marcellus Allen**

WHO SHOT YA 1-3
SON OF A DOPE FIEND 1-4
HEAVEN GOT A GHETTO 1&2
SKI MASK MONEY 1&2
By **Renta**

GORILLAZ IN THE BAY 1-4
TEARS OF A GANGSTA 1/&2
3X KRAZY 1&2
STRAIGHT BEAST MODE 1&2
By **DE'KARI**

TRIGGADALE 1-3
MURDA WAS THE CASE 1-3
By **Elijah R. Freeman**

MARRIED TO A BOSS 1-3
By **Destiny Skai & Chris Green**

SLAUGHTER GANG 1-3
RUTHLESS HEART 1-3
By **Willie Slaughter**

GOD BLESS THE TRAPPERS 1-3
THESE SCANDALOUS STREETS 1-3
FEAR MY GANGSTA 1-5
THESE STREETS DON'T LOVE NOBODY 1-2
BURY ME A G 1-5
A GANGSTA'S EMPIRE 1-4
THE DOPEMAN'S BODYGAURD 1&2
THE REALEST KILLAZ 1-3
THE LAST OF THE OGS 1-3
By **Tranay Adams**

KINGZ OF THE GAME 1-7
CRIME BOSS 1-4
By **Playa Ray**

FUK SHYT
By **Blakk Diamond**

DON'T F#CK WITH MY HEART 1&2
By **Linnea**

ADDICTED TO THE DRAMA 1-3
IN THE ARM OF HIS BOSS
By **Jamila**

LOYALTY AIN'T PROMISED 1&2
By **Keith Williams**

FOREVER GANGSTA 1&2
GLOCKS ON SATIN SHEETS 1&2
By **Adrian Dulan**

YAYO 1-4
A SHOOTER'S AMBITION 1&2
BRED IN THE GAME
By **S. Allen**

TRAP GOD 1-3
RICH $AVAGE 1-3
MONEY IN THE GRAVE 1-3
CARTEL MONEY
By **Martell Troublesome Bolden**

TOE TAGZ 1-4
LEVELS TO THIS SHYT 1&2
IT'S JUST ME AND YOU
By **Ah'Million**

KINGPIN DREAMS 1-3
RAN OFF ON DA PLUG
By **Paper Boi Rari**

THE STREETS MADE ME 1-3
By **Larry D. Wright**

CONFESSIONS OF A GANGSTA 1-4
CONFESSIONS OF A JACKBOY 1-3
CONFESSIONS OF A HITMAN
By **Nicholas Lock**

I'M NOTHING WITHOUT HIS LOVE
SINS OF A THUG
TO THE THUG I LOVED BEFORE
A GANGSTA SAVED XMAS
IN A HUSTLER I TRUST
By **Monet Dragun**

FRESH OFF DA PORCH | IRA B.

QUIET MONEY 1-3
THUG LIFE 1-3
EXTENDED CLIP 1&2
A GANGSTA'S PARADISE
By **Trai'Quan**

CAUGHT UP IN THE LIFE 1-3
THE STREETS NEVER LET GO 1-3
By **Robert Baptiste**

NEW TO THE GAME 1-3
MONEY, MURDER & MEMORIES 1-3
By **Malik D. Rice**

THE LIFE OF A HOOD STAR
By **Ca$h & Rashia Wilson**

THE STREETS WILL NEVER CLOSE 1-4
By **K'ajji**

LIFE OF A SAVAGE 1-4
A GANGSTA'S QUR'AN 1-4
MURDA SEASON 1-3
GANGLAND CARTEL 1-3
CHI'RAQ GANGSTAS 1-4
KILLERS ON ELM STREET 1-3
JACK BOYZ N DA BRONX 1-3
A DOPEBOY'S DREAM 1-3
JACK BOYS VS DOPE BOYS 1-3
COKE GIRLZ
COKE BOYS
SOSA GANG 1&2
BRONX SAVAGES
BODYMORE KINGPINS
BLOOD OF A GOON
By **Romell Tukes**

FRESH OFF DA PORCH | IRA B.

CREAM 2-3
THE STREETS WILL TALK
By **Yolanda Moore**

CONCRETE KILLA 1-3
VICIOUS LOYALTY 1-3
By **Kingpen**

THE ULTIMATE SACRIFICE 1-6
KHADIFI
IF YOU CROSS ME ONCE 1-5
ANGEL 1-4
IN THE BLINK OF AN EYE
By **Anthony Fields**

NIGHTMARES OF A HUSTLA 1-3
BLOOD AND GAMES 1&2
By **King Dream**

HARD AND RUTHLESS 1&2
MOB TOWN 251
THE BILLIONAIRE BENTLEYS 1-3
REAL G'S MOVE IN SILENCE
By **Von Diesel**

MOB TIES 1-7
SOUL OF A HUSTLER, HEART OF A KILLER 1-3
GORILLAZ IN THE TRENCHES
By **SayNoMore**

BODYMORE MURDERLAND 1-3
THE BIRTH OF A GANGSTER 1-4
By **Delmont Player**

FOR THE LOVE OF A BOSS 1&2
By **C. D. Blue**

KILLA KOUNTY 1-5
By **Khufu**

MOBBED UP 1-4
THE BRICK MAN 1-5
THE COCAINE PRINCESS 1-10
STEPPERS 1-3
SUPER GREMLIN 1-4
By **King Rio**

MONEY GAME 1&2
By **Smoove Dolla**

A GANGSTA'S KARMA 1-4
By **FLAME**

KING OF THE TRENCHES 1-3
By **GHOST & TRANAY ADAMS**

QUEEN OF THE ZOO 1&2
By **Black Migo**

GRIMEY WAYS 1-3
BETRAYAL OF A G
By **Ray Vinci**

XMAS WITH AN ATL SHOOTER
By **Ca$h & Destiny Skai**

KING KILLA 1&2
By **Vincent "Vitto" Holloway**

BETRAYAL OF A THUG 1&2
By **Fre$h**

FRESH OFF DA PORCH | IRA B.

THE MURDER QUEENS 1-6
By **Michael Gallon**

FOR THE LOVE OF BLOOD 1-4
By **Jamel Mitchell**

HOOD CONSIGLIERE 1&2
NO TIME FOR ERROR
By **Keese**

PROTÉGÉ OF A LEGEND 1&2
LOVE IN THE TRENCHES 1&2
By **Corey Robinson**

THE PLUG'S RUTHLESS DAUGHTER 1&2
By **Tony Daniels**

BORN IN THE GRAVE 1-3
CRIME PAYS 1&2
By **Self Made Tay**

MOAN IN MY MOUTH
By **XTASY**

TORN BETWEEN A GANGSTER AND A
GENTLEMAN
By **J-BLUNT & Miss Kim**

HERE TODAY GONE TOMORROW 1&2
By **Fly Rock**

PILLOW PRINCESS
By **S. Hawkins**

SANCTIFIED AND HORNY
by **XTASY**

WOMEN LIE MEN LIE 1-4
FIFTY SHADES OF SNOW 1-3
STACK BEFORE YOU SPLURGE
GIRLS FALL LIKE DOMINOES
NAÏVE TO THE STREETS
By **ROY MILLIGAN**

LOYALTY IS EVERYTHING 1-3
CITY OF SMOKE 1&2
By **Molotti**

THE BUTTERFLY MAFIA 1-4
SALUTE MY SAVAGERY 1&2
By **Fumiya Payne**

THE LANE 1&2
By **Ken-Ken Spence**

THE PUSSY TRAP 1-5
By **Nene Capri**

DIRTY DNA
By **Blaque**

BOOKS BY LDP'S CEO, CA$H

TRUST IN NO MAN
TRUST IN NO MAN 2
TRUST IN NO MAN 3
BONDED BY BLOOD
SHORTY GOT A THUG
THUGS CRY
THUGS CRY 2
THUGS CRY 3
TRUST NO BITCH
TRUST NO BITCH 2
TRUST NO BITCH 3
TIL MY CASKET DROPS
RESTRAINING ORDER
RESTRAINING ORDER 2
IN LOVE WITH A CONVICT
LIFE OF A HOOD STAR
XMAS WITH AN ATL SHOOTER

www.ingramcontent.com/pod-product-compliance
Lightning Source LLC
Chambersburg PA
CBHW070455260626
47161CB00004B/1317